Think of Me
Tangled Up
Careless Whisper
Please Remember Me
What Might Have Been
Ever Fallen In Love
Savin' Me
Someone Like You
Over My Head
Love Remembers

WHEN YOU'RE WITH ME

WENDI ZWADUK

When You're With Me
ISBN # 978-0-85715-985-4
©Copyright Wendi Zwaduk 2012
Cover Art by Lyn Taylor ©Copyright March 2012
Interior text design by Claire Siemaszkiewicz
Total-E-Bound Publishing

This is a work of fiction. All characters, places and events are from the author's imagination and should not be confused with fact. Any resemblance to persons, living or dead, events or places is purely coincidental.

All rights reserved. No part of this publication may be reproduced in any material form, whether by printing, photocopying, scanning or otherwise without the written permission of the publisher, Total-E-Bound Publishing.

Applications should be addressed in the first instance, in writing, to Total-E-Bound Publishing. Unauthorised or restricted acts in relation to this publication may result in civil proceedings and/or criminal prosecution.

The author and illustrator have asserted their respective rights under the Copyright Designs and Patents Acts 1988 (as amended) to be identified as the author of this book and illustrator of the artwork.

Published in 2011 by Total-E-Bound Publishing, Think Tank, Ruston Way, Lincoln, LN6 7FL, United Kingdom.

No part of this book may be reproduced, scanned, or distributed in any printed or electronic form without permission. Please do not participate in or encourage piracy of copyrighted materials in violation of the authors' rights. Purchase only authorised copies.

Total-E-Bound Publishing is an imprint of Total-E-Ntwined Limited.

If you purchased this book without a cover you should be aware that this book is stolen property. It was reported as "unsold and destroyed" to the publisher and neither the author nor the publisher has received any payment for this "stripped book".

WHEN YOU'RE WITH ME

To Kelly —
Enjoy the read
& hope you write
your story, too!

2012

Dedication

N—for making me get this book back out after I'd shelved it.
E—for reading it when it was the first rough draft.
A—always good to have a lawyer in the house.
SB—for having faith in me and being fantastic.
JPZ—when you're with me, I feel like I can do anything. I love you.

Prologue

"Nine-one-one. Please state your emergency."

Jude hugged her knees and rocked on the floor of her art studio. Instead of the art supplies, all she saw was the vision from behind the club earlier. Her hands trembled as she clutched her cell phone. The memory of the blood, the smell... Her stomach lurched and bile filled her mouth.

"Nine-one-one. Your emergency, please?"

"I'd like to report a murder." Jude blinked and drew a long breath into her lungs. She needed to calm down or she'd never make it through the call. Tears burned behind her eyes. She shouldn't have been in hiding. She needed to be right there with her friend.

"Okay, can you give me the location?"

"Thirteen hundred Broadway. Behind the Silver Steel."

"Silver Steel gentlemen's club?"

"Yes." She closed her eyes and once again the vision gripped her. She'd only been asked to dump Astra's things. *Astra ran off to Vegas with Slade. She's not coming back. Just pitch her trash.* She bit back the sour taste of vomit in her mouth. Tiny had never asked her to dump trash before. That was Corey's job.

"Ma'am?"

"I'm sorry." Jude cleared her throat. The best thing to do was just to explain what she'd seen. "I took out the garbage behind the club and, when I opened the compactor, there was a hand."

"A hand?"

Jude nodded. How in the world did the dispatcher manage to stay so calm? "Yes. My friend Astra Devlin and her boyfriend Slade McMann were supposed to have gone to Vegas, but they didn't."

"And how do you know, ma'am?"

"Because it was her hand in the compactor." Jude rocked back and forth. The vision of the hand remained crisp in her mind—bloody and reaching towards the opening to the compactor. The smell of rot and decay held fast as well. Her stomach lurched again.

"We've got a unit on the way. Can you give me your name?"

Her name? *Oh shit.* Jude trembled. If she gave her name, her boss would know who had alerted the cops. If she'd been confident enough to tell them her name, she'd never have run from the scene straight to the safety of her studio.

She stared at her cell phone, unsure of what to do.

"Ma'am?"

Jude snapped the phone shut and gave it a fling across the room. If the cops wanted her badly enough, they'd no doubt find her. She'd seen enough crime dramas to know the police had a lot of tricks for finding people.

Just as long as her boss didn't find out. If he remained in the dark, she'd be safe. *If.*

Chapter One

"I need a lover who will drive me crazy in all the right ways..."

Detective Drew Alwyn tapped his pen to the beat of the song in his head while he waited for Lieutenant Wallace to begin the briefing session.

In his twelve years with the Carrington Falls Police Department in Ohio, Drew had never imagined being alone. Wasn't a cop supposed to have a good woman to come home to? The next time he walked into his apartment, a wilted spider plant would offer the only comfort, and Drew wasn't the type to talk to greenery.

The scent of day-old coffee and industrial cleaner wafted into the cramped, grey discussion room. Drew rubbed his stomach to quell the rumbling. Coffee sounded awful, but a sandwich sounded so good—something with roast beef and cheese. When had he eaten last? The club sandwich at eleven-thirty. He flicked his wrist to check the time on his thick watch. Five-fifteen. Damn.

He grabbed the bottle of soda from his backpack and uncapped it, then took a long draw. The sugar wouldn't quiet his hunger, but the caffeine would keep him awake when he ventured on duty in an hour. He took a pen from his notebook, clicked the button at the top and began doodling. The sound of conversation in the hallway did nothing to take his mind off the undercover operation or the death of his friend and colleague, Sergeant Randy McCall.

Drew's partner, a bear of a red-haired man named James Mateo, strolled into the room and sat down in the closest chair. "You ready for this one?"

Drew looked up from his sketch. "This one what? We knew the bastard couldn't stay underground for long. We just gotta prove he's the one who took McCall down and put him in the dumpster." He shuddered thinking about the photos of Randy hacked up and left to rot behind the gentlemen's club.

James crossed his legs and flipped open his notepad. "True. Randy was one hell of an officer, even if he chose the damn stupid name of Slade as a cover. Tiny's always looking to make a quick buck. You think he's shaking down the girls? It was a stroke of genius to send you and Nester in as customers. You know the lay of the so-called land and Tiny thinks you're clean. As clean as a bouncer in a strip club can be."

Drew added some details to his drawing and frowned. The woman in the sketch had begun to take on the features of the elusive female from down the hallway in his decoy apartment building. The soft-spoken brunette with the sparkling ice-blue eyes. The girl who lugged the enormous art portfolio down to the parking lot each morning. The one whose smile warmed his heart on the coldest evenings. The one woman he wanted to get to know better, preferably naked…and she had no idea.

He ground his teeth together. With this new undercover operation, any meeting with the sweet-natured female was out of the question. At least, not under the pretence of the truth.

"Is she your new girlfriend?"

Drew crinkled his brows. "No. I can't get with her."

James elbowed Drew's ribs. "Why the hell not? If she's as hot as your scribble there, then you'd better hit that."

Drew shook his head. "I can't get involved while undercover. You know the rules as well as I do. Plus, if Carlie found out she'd kill me."

James slapped the pad on the wooden desk. "Bullshit. She walked away from you to screw around with Troy Balleswicz over in Vice. She doesn't deserve your second chances. So what's this chick's name?"

Drew tossed his pen onto his own graffiti-decorated desk. "You're right. I don't owe Carlie anything, but Wallace put her in the Silver Steel as one of the dancers — Gold Dust Woman, if I'm not mistaken. If I get the security detail, then I gotta work with her. She'll make life hell for any other female in my life. I don't need that kind of crap right now."

James folded his arms. "You didn't answer my question. What's Scribble's real name?"

"I'm not sure what her real name is. They have stage names." Drew raked his fingers through his hair. "I still haven't worked up the nerve to speak to her. She's quiet and always on the move. I can't pin her down unless she's at the club and I don't want to spook her by coming off as a pervert or another guy wanting to cop a quick feel." He averted his gaze from Mateo. "Trust me... If I could, I would ask this girl for a private dance."

Lieutenant Frank Wallace strolled into the room with retired Detective Ross Malsam in tow. James dug his elbow into Drew's ribs again. "When this is all over, you got a month of vacation time coming. Why not hunt her down and tag that?"

Drew frowned. "Tag that? How about I just learn her name and see what happens from there?"

Wallace cleared his throat. "If you're done chatting, ladies, I called you two in here for the Silver Steel operation."

James shrugged and grabbed a pen and notebook from his bag.

Drew groaned and half-listened to the directive. His dream girl ruled his brain.

"Gentlemen, the drug problem in the west end is getting worse. After the discovery of McCall's body, we're not taking chances. Salazar 'Tiny' Balthazar's targeting the girls in the exotic clubs. Two are missing and one is confirmed dead. Alwyn, I want you to work the security detail as a transfer from the Pink Pussy Cat Club in Chatsworth. Kenworth supplied me with a list of the dancers and Malsam has given me the accompanying photographs."

Ross Malsam handed each detective a manila folder. The former officer swept his comb-over across his forehead and frowned. His brown eyes darkened. "Drew, Tiny knows your reputation from the PPC and wants you personally. He's always got something up his sleeve, so keep on your guard double time. I lost McCall. I don't want to replace you too. Mateo, you'll come in for an interview tonight as a bartender. Harry's looking forward to the help. Questions?"

Drew flipped through the stack of pictures. Most of the women wore too much makeup. Their hair fluffed around their faces. Forced smiles painted their lips. He knew each girl and their particular dance styles, not that he cared. He rolled his eyes until he came to the last image. His breath caught fast in his throat.

Mateo elbowed Drew. "That's your girl. According to the dossier, her stage name is Judy Blue Eyes, but her real name is Jude Nelson. Looks like a sweet thing. Innocent, ya know?"

Drew shook his head and drank in her details. Kohl-rimmed blue eyes sparkled and her pale skin shone with the honest smile on her crimson lips. Ringlets cascaded from the crown of her head and swathed her pink-tinged cheeks. "She looks too innocent to work in such a dive."

"I'm sorry, Alwyn. Is there a conflict?" Wallace asked. "You have the best inside information on this operation. McCall was your friend. If you have any issues, then you need to get out now. Your work as Ramon Decker is essential."

Drew closed the folder. He glanced at Ross. "No conflict. I'll be fine. It's just different to see the dancers I pretended to ogle as real people." Sure, he'd be fine if he could stay a decent distance from Jude. A voice in the back of his mind didn't agree.

She's your salvation.

As Wallace returned to his directive, Drew slipped Jude's photo from the folder. He prayed she didn't remember him and, if she did, he hoped she wasn't involved in the drug ring. He needed to trust one insider.

Or maybe he simply wanted her.

Shit.

An hour later, Drew headed out of the office and into the parking garage. He craved space, speed and chrome in order to get into character as Ramon Decker—bouncer and all-around hard-ass.

"I am Ramon," he chanted. "I am Ramon, the bouncer and tough guy extraordinaire. I have to believe it so they'll believe it."

Instead of the elevators, Drew chose the exercise and fresher air of the stairwell. His days as a beat cop had enticed him with wide-open spaces and room to move. Now that he'd become a detective, he coveted his freedom—it reminded him of his time on the farm when he'd had no commitments. He liked having space to work within the team, though, rather than carrying the entire load on his shoulders as he had as a child.

When he opened the door to the second level, his cell phone rang. He knew the ring tone—Carlie Kenworth, his most recent ex-girlfriend. He stopped on the landing to answer her call. Since their acrimonious split six months ago, he'd refused to talk to her and she ignored him unless she wanted something. Now, circumstances were forcing them to work together and get along.

He used his cold, authoritative voice. "This is Alwyn."

Carlie was the type of woman who never knew when to give up and walk away, especially when she was the one to cause the problems. Carlie hated competition. He couldn't forget that her jealous streak was a country mile wide and violent. Although she was a stunning woman with statuesque legs, perfectly coiffed bleached blonde hair and high cheekbones, her downfall was her selfishness.

He didn't have time for her shenanigans. A raw shiver ran the length of his spine. Bile rose in his throat. Carlie had a tendency of showing up when he least expected her…like right then.

She giggled. "I know who you are, silly."

"What do you want, Carlie?"

"Are you alone?"

"Nope." He leaned on the wall of the parking garage.

On her end of the line, she snorted. "Who are you with? Anyone I should know?" The question served as a thinly veiled reference to the reason they'd split up—she'd cheated on him with another officer on the police force.

Drew glanced through the window in the steel door out at his motorcycle. It was a used Harley that had needed restorative work when he'd bought it. After his brand of TLC, the machine gleamed like it was brand new. It was his pride and joy.

"You've never met," he said smoothly. *And you never will...*

"Can you come over?"

He gritted his teeth. "Are you drunk? We have a major case going that you can't screw up because you're angry."

"I'm just looking for a good time before we go back undercover."

Drew rolled his eyes. "Carlie, honey, we broke up. You didn't want me then, but now you do? Look, I'm a good detective, but I need a few clues. What's changed?"

"I can admit my mistakes," she purred. "Letting you go was my biggest. You're a great catch and a compassionate lover."

"I see. Why do you *really* want me there?"

So she could rip out his heart and stomp it into the floor? Or maybe sleep with a co-worker and then laugh because he'd taken offence? Yeah, he felt sorry that she was lonely, but not that he'd walked away. A man could only take so much emotional abuse.

"I'm making martinis and thought you could share the drinks with me. I've been lonely without you."

"Really?"

"I want to reconnect with *you*. We had such great times together and I miss the way you made me scream. No one has ever been able to match you—not even Troy."

Drew rolled his eyes again. He'd made her scream all right. She'd screamed from when he'd walked in the door until the minute he'd walked back out. Her language made the most vulgar individuals look tame by comparison. She could just stick with the other officer—he'd had enough.

"Well... Think about it." She blew a kiss into the phone.

Drew groaned. "Much as I like your company, I'll pass."

"But—"

He cut off any further argument when he snapped the phone shut and slipped it into his jacket pocket. "I know I have to work with her, but I really need to block her personal calls."

Drew took a breath of fresh air. As he burst through the parking garage door, three rows of vehicles ranging from family to sleek sports cars belonging to his co-workers welcomed him like silent sentries. Silence was exactly what he desired after the irritating call from Carlie.

The early September evening was cool and almost abrasive on his skin. The setting sun gave the chrome on the bike an orange glow. He sat astride the leather seat and gripped the handlebars. Being on the bike made him feel powerful and sexy. Drew needed to feel manly and desired. *Jude.* She brought out his virility. He revved the engine. She stirred him, and yet she was the one woman he couldn't pursue. The situation reminded him of something his buddy Ned used to say.

What kind of fool messes up a good thing?
A man with a dick for brains.

Drew laughed without humour at the pun and took in the sights of the main drag to clear his mind. He wasn't afraid of women—quite the opposite. He liked most women. But the *right* woman, the one who turned his world inside out, didn't seem to exist.

Was there any woman who could love him without screwing him over? He'd had Nat, Wren, and Carlie... None of those women had flipped the switch. They had labelled him a failure and a cold-hearted man. After so much rejection, he'd begun to believe he would end up alone, like his father.

He tried to dislodge the depressive thoughts in his head. Forget women and relationships—look at the scenery and blend into the job.

Drew considered the buildings and neighbourhoods of his home town. Closed restaurants, lumbering factory buildings and abandoned furniture stores littered the area. He shook his head. The big box retail shops had moved out to the more prosperous edge of town, leaving the main city to decay. What had been a booming urban area thirty years prior was now a sad, empty and dilapidated shell of its former self. Green space was at a severe premium.

Economic healing? Not here... Concrete and crime were everywhere. All of which he remembered clearly from his beat cop days.

Drew's humour masked his unhappiness. Just like his birthplace, he felt like a broken-down shell of his younger self. Used and abused.

He remembered when Carrington Falls had been a thriving area for oil and steel. Now it looked like a sad excuse for a ghost town with all the buildings boarded up or turned into seedy bars and strip clubs. It was cold and distant, just like his heart. So much for being a warm place to raise a family, like it used to be. Not anymore. He couldn't make himself feel what wasn't there.

Drew swung his long legs off the bike and turned to the setting sun. The slight warmth heated his face. Determination coiled around his brain as he locked the bike in the storage unit and strode towards the Nissan across the parking lot. For Randy and the other fallen officers, he'd nail the murderer and shut down the drug ring. "I am Ramon Decker and I'm here for the job of bouncer."

With renewed spirit, Drew became Ramon and drove the battered black car to the strip club. He was a regular customer and tonight he'd become a part of the inner group. *Time for sex with no strings or feelings — just cold distant sex and hot chicks willing to shake it. Time to kiss up to the bad guy so I can stick his ass in jail.*

He walked along the crumbling black asphalt of the parking lot, past the cool red brick façade and neon signs shouting *Girls, Girls, Girls,* and *XXX Shows,* into the foyer of the Silver Steel. *Here's to the next benchmark in my life.*

* * * *

Jude Nelson stood at the back of the dressing room and stretched in front of the mirror. Nude except for the flesh-coloured thong, she proceeded to examine every inch of her body to see what she could manipulate on stage to be sexier. In her opinion, she saw a plain woman with average looks.

Jude knew she wasn't exactly the ideal specimen for an exotic dancer. Diminutive at a mere five feet two inches, she sported size C breasts and curvy hips. Far from fat, she saw herself as voluptuous in a smaller package.

She squared her shoulders and pouted her lips. "I have confidence. Dancing tonight will put me ahead three more tuition payments and maybe I'll get to see the hunk."

Jude tossed her hair over her shoulder. "Maybe a high ponytail with lots of curls. That might look extra hot," she murmured to herself. She turned her head to examine her hair at another angle and frowned. What about a sleek look?

She frowned again. Without the right sexy look, the night would be long and especially rough for a Friday. Rough nights equalled paltry tips and unpaid bills. Jude wouldn't starve, but the poverty level beckoned. She needed a good night.

"Stop staring at yourself and get dressed," Renee Walker shouted, startling Jude. "You're being vain. You go on in half an hour. I want you to surf the crowd once you're done. You need to circulate more, so I can get my money's worth out of you. It's Thursday, so be on the point. You'll appreciate the tips."

Jude arched her brow at the self-appointed housemother and former dancer.

Vain? She described it as 'attempting to be sexier than humanly possible'...definitely not vain. If Renee thought her actions to be vain, then she was sorely mistaken.

Fine. I'll prove you wrong. I am sexy.

Jude knew full well that Renee wasn't the gentlest of women. With a flame-red teased wig, dark brown eyebrows, heavily painted-on eyeliner and thin wrinkled lips, she wasn't in her prime any longer. Her wide hips and perpetual grimace did nothing to improve her approachability. She'd been batted around by life and wasn't afraid to slap back at anyone who got in her way. Many times she'd kicked at anyone who'd dared just to look at her wrong. It was a means of protection so she'd never get hurt. Her temper was notorious...with Jude as her usual target.

Today was no exception.

"You don't really bring in the customers like you should." She swatted Jude's ass with an echoing crack. "You only have a few assets, so try to work them hard. Use the pasties tonight. Anything has to help your looks—God knows I can't."

Jude nodded and turned to the dressing table to apply the heavy stage makeup. She didn't want to wear the pasties or step in front of that crowd. She'd prefer to wear a turtleneck and jeans, or at least her art smock, and be comfortable. She wanted respect as a true artist, not a working girl who took her clothes off for money.

But that was fodder for another day. Tonight she would shine. She had no other choice. Jude stepped into the tearaway dress and fumbled with the zipper.

Just then, Andie showed up to help. She tugged at the bodice of the gown Jude wore and spit out a string of indiscernible curse words. "Why don't you go without a bodice for once? I'm having a hell of a time getting you into this one." Andie spoke close to Jude's ear. "Don't drink your bottled water. Tiny slipped you something."

Jude frowned at her reflection. "I'm fine. I think this outfit will become my speciality. You know, pop out and break out?" She dropped her head. "Thanks."

Outwardly, Jude reeked of confidence. She had to. Any show of fear and the clientele would know it. If the dancer displayed anything less than full confidence, her tips drastically declined.

Jude couldn't afford it. The need to keep a roof over her head trumped her self-esteem. She had art supplies to purchase and a degree to finish. *Do whatever you need to survive and rise above* — that was her motto.

Inwardly, she was a pile of cowardly mush. Unlike many of her fellow dancers, Jude never got a rush or an orgasm from dancing. She tried her best to block out what she did and any sensation she gleaned from it, to be a robot.

Jude sighed and glanced at her helper. At twenty-nine, Andie Martin personified the American girl — long legs, natural blonde hair, and a smile that lit the darkest room. Her green eyes sparkled with a lethal combination of sexuality and mischief. Good thing Jude didn't have a man — he'd drop her for Andie in a hot minute. At least she and the willowy model-type were friends.

"There… I got you in it. Now go out there and pop out of it," Andie puffed. "Knock 'em dead, kiddo."

Jude peeked down at her squashed breasts and sighed again. The fiery red antebellum outfit with the Velcro tear-away skirt wasn't her shtick, but it was a crowd-pleaser so she'd caved to Renee's earlier request.

"Okay, I'll give it more than my best shot," she replied and winked at Andie. "Time to dazzle." What a lie! Dancing merely paid the bills. That's all she'd let it be — a quick blip on the radar to reaching her dreams. Personal feelings didn't matter if she could keep the tuition up to date.

She turned her back on the double row of makeup tables, dirty maroon carpet and crusty, faux-wood panelled walls, held her head high and stepped up the ramp to the stage.

Be a machine. Wasn't that what Jolene said? Then no one gets hurt... Parents won't pass judgment or set unrealistic standards. Friends won't run because of less than stellar living conditions. Men won't know the truth because they can't get close enough to find out. Strippers were the lowest life form, weren't they?

Rise above. What doesn't kill me makes me stronger.

Jude swallowed hard and summoned her courage. She had to become Judy Blue Eyes.

I am beautiful.

As soon as Jude got into position, butterflies flooded her stomach. The red patent-leather stilettos nearly gave out beneath her. It happened every time she prepared to dance because it was the only time she couldn't hide her emotions — hide her fear. She could do this.

Jude resorted to her tried and true pep talk while she adjusted her dress.

Think about class. This is one step closer to the studio degree. It's one step closer to becoming a professional artist. No matter what they say, I am beautiful.

The curtain opened and Jude began her dance. She marched out on to the empty stage where she began to shimmy on the pole as though she liked what she was doing. Her stomach roiled. Her cool expression and tight smile masked her embarrassment.

Tables surrounded the stage in the cavernous but dimly lit room. The DJ stood in a booth to the right of the stage, supplying the music to the dancers and serving as a last-defence bouncer in the event of trouble.

Jude normally chose slow, sexually charged blues songs with a lot of bass because she could better time her movements to the beat. Tonight she was trying a country hit she'd recently heard. The DJ added a thumping techno bass line. The song then became easy to lose herself in and let go. Her hands roamed her body, while her hips shifted to the seductive rhythm. At least her own actions made her feel something.

Jude noticed the men bunch against the stage. They seemed drawn to her movements. The more she touched her breasts and moved her ass in time to the sexy beat, the better her tips became. What would this feel like with a man? Instinct dictated that it would sparkle. When she ripped away the full skirt, the crowd went wild.

"I won't expect a tomorrow when we have no guaranteed today," the singer sang. *"I'll love you like there's no tomorrow and hide within your fire."*

Jude agreed. Her heart still ached—she longed for a tomorrow and a man whose fire was worthy of hiding in. There, she could belong and feel safe—a place to call home and arms open only for her. Did that exist?

She doubted it.

Maybe someday.

Chapter Two

At his private table, Ramon ordered a beer and stretched out, expecting the same old, same old — world-weary women who cared less about taking their clothes off and more about how much he was willing to put in their g-strings.

He laced his hands behind his head. Thirty or so tables ringed the phallus-shaped stage. To his mild surprise, a handful of women joined the male-dominated crowd. The bar lined the left wall with two smaller circle stages for wild Friday and Saturday nights. A combination of body heat and cigarette smoke hung thick in the air.

Instead of watching the girl on stage, he surveyed the landscape. Martin Nester — another officer — sat in the corner smoking a cigarette. Clint Robison stood by the bar with a beer chilling in his hand. As Ramon had expected, Carlie giggled on the lap of a middle-aged male patron. Other girls flitted around the room, fetching drinks and entertaining men in the crowd.

Another dancer, whose name he couldn't remember, sauntered by with a handful of condoms. She fanned them out like a deck of cards. "Interested?"

He gave her a smooth smile and shook his head once. "Not tonight, honey."

She winked and continued to her destination across the room. According to the findings of the police force, the Silver Steel offered massage services, but not call girls. Why the condoms? And what did they have to do with the drug trade at the club? Ramon searched the room for Ross, his connection.

When the next dancer stepped out on to the stage, Ramon forgot all about his mission. His hands fell limply into his lap. He knew what strippers looked like. Hell, he'd arrested enough of them while he'd been out on the beat to know that they were a jaded bunch. Shake a little, get the money by the bucket-load, and get out before any attachments formed—that was their way of life.

This woman was exactly his type. She had an air of sexuality and innocence about her that, in his heart, he knew was real. There was no front about her. She was the type of girl that he could see living next door in his apartment building. Some women tried to be sweet, but she was the real thing. Vulnerability and innate sexuality shone on her face and stirred something in his belly. Was it desire? This wasn't the first time he'd watched her dance, but this was the first time he'd felt something. Hell if he knew why. He'd lusted after his former wife Natalie, but that was nothing compared to how he felt now. He assumed it was just super-sized lust. Couldn't be anything more…

He continued to stare—this girl was someone rare. He needed to get over his damned shyness and meet her. She was solely responsible for his instant boner.

Hell, he'd nearly got off just looking at her. What ripped right through to his soul were her blue eyes. There was a piercing, examining quality in them that resonated deep into his being and sent a jolt of heat straight to his cock. His hands twitched with the overwhelming need to touch and protect her. What would her lips taste like? Would she be as soft as she looked?

Totally out of his withdrawn character, Ramon stopped his waitress and slipped her a five. "I want a private dance."

The waitress bent down, slid the money into her bodice, and spoke in his ear. "I'll send a note to the bar. Harry sets it up from there. Who's the lucky girl?"

Ramon looked directly at the stage and nodded. "Her." A wicked grin curled his lips. She caught his fancy, twisted it upside down, and turned it into desire with just one look. Everyone else in the room evaporated. *I need to meet her. She looks like she could take my mind off my troubles for a little while...*

"Judy Blue Eyes is a good choice, but she rarely agrees. She's shy."

Through his peripheral vision, Ramon noticed the waitress giving him a slow once-over. Her eyes rested on the bulge in his jeans. He didn't cotton to the visual groping—it would have diverted his concentration from the dancer and his job. The waitress would have to wait for another willing partner.

She brought her gaze to his. "You might be able to cut through her defences."

Ramon's attention returned to Judy Blue Eyes. *Jude.* She was magnetic and sensuous without really trying. He felt like she'd touched his core without touching him at all—it was critical that he reciprocate.

Jude stared right at him and smiled as if they shared a private joke. A blush crept over her body. She licked her lips and turned in his direction. Ramon wondered if she thought about him as she touched her body. The corner of her mouth crooked up again. He'd spent many a night fantasising about her. The more he observed Jude, the more he liked what he saw. The more he liked, the more his feelings of need scared him shitless.

A little while might not be long enough... Maybe longer...if the impending drug bust didn't get in the way.

It was a third of the way through the song before Jude bothered to look at her audience. Focusing on the crowd was one of her no-nos because, when she saw their faces, she lost a little of her nerve. It was always the same bunch of middle-aged men whose bellies stuck out over their belts. They had wives and ex-wives. Too many were drunk or wanted drugs. Not exactly her idea of hot guys, even if they were willing to pay for her presentation. There's no tomorrow out there. That's always a given.

As with the song, tonight was the night for exceptions. Tonight, she ignored her fear and looked out into the audience. Tiny, with his biochemical design tattooed on the side of his head and tribal tattoo ringing his neck, roamed through the crowd. He gave her the creeps each time he came out on to the club floor. At least he paid her no attention—he preferred blondes.

On the other side of the room, Jude saw a man worthy of entertaining—her mystery male. The desire to touch her body became real and overwhelming. The blond hunk was familiar, smouldering, and appeared attainable—a deadly combination. Almost as though at his mental request, the snaps capturing her breasts in the bodice popped open, revealing two of her best assets.

Forget fear...hello visual orgasm.

Jude's lips parted and a flush came over her body. She gazed longingly at the stranger sitting at table thirty-two. Even through the smoke that clouded the distance, she could see a slight sparkle in his eye. That glint gave her the courage to be much bolder than she'd ever been before. She'd noticed him before, but tonight he looked on edge and intense. He had his hands behind his head, but dropped them as she watched. His focus was on her—only her.

She wanted to touch him—to caress and fondle...to see what made him tick and explore new worlds. Did he feel the same? Muscles flexed under his shirt as he moved. Did he have a hairy chest or was it smooth? She bet they would fit together like a matched set.

Wow, where'd that thought come from?

More turned on than she'd ever been in her life, Jude wondered if he could see her sopping wet excitement. *Could see it? But he wasn't supposed to!* Yeah, he seemed like a decent guy, but there must be a story. A cheating wife? A loveless marriage? A girlfriend who was out of town? Maybe he was the type that could only do it with a hooker. The desire to hate him as she did the others was inexplicably missing.

In the forefront of her mind, she danced for his private pleasure. She touched her breasts and plucked at her nipples, making them taut. He nodded, seeming to approve. Would he like to lick them? Would he like to explore everywhere else?

Jude shivered. She wanted to learn his name and everything about him. She gyrated with the music, rarely taking her eyes away from his. The only remaining parts of her costume were her thong and red stilettos. He gripped his beer bottle in a white-knuckled fist. His gaze raked up and down her body. Dear Lord, she wanted to show him everything. Could he be the man to teach her what sex should be like?

It felt naughty, but Jude liked his heated gaze. She tilted her head back and teased her fingers down her neck. Lust radiated between her legs. He'd created the sensations without even touching her.

Now she saw how Jolene claimed she got off while dancing.

If all the clients were like him, this would be so much easier...so much more exciting.

She rubbed her ass up and down the pole then arched her back as the music faded away. Any question as to how she felt disappeared with her apprehension. Jude made a decision that was totally out of character. She knew where to circulate.

* * * *

The waitress returned with Tiny Balthazar in tow. Ramon bit back a grimace and forced a tight smile. The pungent scent of Tiny's aftershave cut through the thick smoke wafting through the room.

Tiny sat on the chair next to Ramon. The wooden legs screeched against the tile floor. "You like my club, I see."

Ramon sipped his beer. "I appreciate beautiful women."

Tiny folded his meaty, tattooed arms. "Ross tells me you are in search of a job, Mr Decker. I saw your work at the Pink Pussy and I want you. I have a business proposition that would make us both happy. I want you to keep the drunks in line, and you can ogle the girls all you want."

Ramon nodded. "Taking out the trash is one of my specialities."

"That's what I wanted to hear. I need good men to keep things in line." Tiny chuckled and wrapped his arm around the waitress. "According to Charisma, here, you have an interest in Judy Blue Eyes." He glanced over his shoulder at the empty stage. "She's one of our rare girls. She doesn't entertain many clients on a personal scale, but she does seem to bring men in looking for an attainable girl next door. Judy makes pudge sell."

"You said it." Ramon cocked a brow to stifle his disdain. Although Jude was indeed pretty, he wasn't sure he liked hearing the dealer refer to her as attainable and he sure as hell refused to label her as a pudge. The asshole.

Tiny handed Ramon a card and smirked. "Go to the black door next to the bar. It says private, but if you show Harry your card he'll let you through. My treat, since you're now on the payroll." He stood and smoothed his silk shirt. "Somehow, I have the feeling you'll be just what she wants, or needs, and, since I encourage my bouncers to engage in personal relationships with my dancers, you two might be good for each other. See me in my office when you're finished. I'll have Goldie give you the grand tour."

Ramon raised a brow. "Goldie?"

"Miranda — AKA Gold Dust Woman. I like the girls to use song title stage names. It's my special touch." With that, Tiny strolled away, smoking his cigar and leaving puffs of smoke in his wake.

As much as his common sense told Ramon to back out and stay unattached, his groin and his duty to the force told him to stay put. He had to see Jude. He needed her to be real and not an image on the stage. Her breasts, her hips, her face...and those eyes... Dear God, he needed her—every bit of her. And, if getting to her meant dealing with Carlie as Miranda AKA Goldie, challenge accepted.

Ramon made his way to the black door next to the bar. He nodded at the raven-haired bartender, who immediately came over. The man was at least six inches shorter than Ramon, but over-wrought with solid, angry muscle.

"Where are you going?" Harry's voice was gruff. He held out a meaty hand.

"Got a directive from the boss." Fear and exhilaration flowed through his veins. Jude would be worth the hassle. He just hoped he could still see her after the shit hit the proverbial fan.

Ramon watched Harry give the paper the once-over and nod at the door. "You get half an hour, courtesy of Mr Balthazar." The bartender held out his hand. "You must've made an impression. Are you the new muscle?"

"Something like that. I'm supposed to remove the disorderlies and keep the place under control."

"Ross picked you?"

"Sure did. I worked the Pink Pussy Cat Club over in Chatsworth until they closed last month."

"Lucky for you. Pussy Cat wasn't the safest place to work." Harry rubbed the patch of thick black hair covering his chin. "You get room number two. Go in and sit. She'll come in through the back door. Rules... She can touch you, but you can't touch her without her permission. No sex—oral or otherwise. If there's a problem, we got bouncers watching the cameras in each room." He unlocked the thick door. "Since you're

Mr Balthazar's guest, you can do as you please, as long as she agrees. She screams, then I'll personally kick your ass outta here. Got it?"

Ramon nodded. He hadn't come here to break the rules. Well…not all the rules and not just yet. He passed through the gateway and located room two in the harshly lit hallway. A ripple of anticipation and wanton desire wracked his body. He replayed her dance in his head. What had she done that was so special? He'd watched her flit around the main room serving drinks and charming customers. Every gyration and caress had stirred his libido.

Ramon turned the knob on the door. One leather armchair, one faux-leather covered bench, a silver pole and a very obvious camera decorated the room. He chuckled. "Must make it easy to hose down at closing time," he muttered.

Ramon took his seat and waited. He perched on the edge of the chair, on guard for every sound and hint of movement. Chalk it up to rigorous academy training. As a cop, he needed to be aware and cautious. As a man, he felt he needed to be in control. Now he knew how suspects felt while awaiting interrogation—scared to death. Despite the severity of the situation, a ripple of desire ripped through him. She stirred his libido. For Miss Judy Blue Eyes, he'd be aware, but she could have all the control. Nothing good ever lasted in his life. He wanted to enjoy her, and the ride, for as long as possible.

Jude considered grumbling when Renee told her about the private dance. She didn't like being alone with the clients. She hated the feeling of being in danger. Plus, it was going to prevent her from finding her mystery man.

After an upbraiding from Renee, Jude relented and found a black demi-bra, which she paired with a black thong. For concealment, she slid into a man's crisp, white dress shirt. It felt like her art smock, which gave her confidence. She desperately needed something to make her feel strong in this situation. She stepped into a pair of black stilettos and finger-combed her hair. Checking her look in the mirror wasn't going to happen. She needed more than conviction to get through this.

"I have got to find a better job," she muttered as she walked to the door. In her mind, she concocted an image of a large man with terrible body odour, blunt fingers, rough stubble and bad breath. He would want to manhandle her to get his way. Why did her nightmares seem to become real? Jude shook and fisted her hands. She took a deep breath and turned the knob. *Let him be...decent.*

Jude leaned against the doorframe to size up her situation. The client sat on the green leather chair. In person, he didn't appear to be as menacing as the figment she'd built up in her mind. Actually, he was sexy and familiar...

Her brain finally registered who he was...her mystery man!

She knew the bleached-blond stud with the smouldering chocolate brown eyes couldn't possibly be here to see her. He had gorgeous women like Andie and Colleen falling at his feet. Why lower himself to her level? She felt so plain, chunky and average by comparison. Maybe this was her chance. He turned her on just by sitting in the room. Could he be interested in her?

She shut the door and backed against it to hide her quaking knees. He was gorgeous...and she wondered what his ulterior motives could be. Men like him always told her to 'get a real job'. They explained that she was way out of their league and only gave her attention in pity.

Still, her mouth watered. The man personified strength and sensuality, from his well-worn motorcycle boots to his shaggy bleached hair. Here was the man she'd quietly lusted after for the past couple of months, and he'd paid money to see *her*—no freakin' way! *All I had to do was invite him in for a lap dance?* Inadvertently, she clutched her hand to her chest. Her nipples went taut and desire pooled low in her belly. She wanted to caress herself and turn him on as much as he did her. What was he thinking? Her lips parted, dying for a taste of her dream man.

The hunk did something that totally shocked Jude—he smiled. It wasn't mean or evil, but genuine, warm and natural. He looked happy to be here. Beguiling...like he wanted her.

He spoke first, breaking the heavy silence. "Are you Miss Judy Blue Eyes?"

Jude nodded. His husky baritone made her crazy and warmed her entire body. What if he shouted her name? She had to get a grip before he walked out. "I'm Judy...er...Jude." She hated her stage name. It came from a pretty rock song, but it didn't describe who she was. Not that her name mattered much. Once he'd found out that she was damaged goods, he'd walk away in a heartbeat. Normal girls don't take their clothes off for money. She was far from normal.

"I'm one of Tiny's new hired guns, Ramon Decker. What do I get for my trouble, sweet girl?"

His question brought her back to reality. The sound of his voice soothed away her fears, although her common sense warned her to be cautious. He didn't push, assume, or try to grab her as she would have expected. The sexy smile continued to curl his lips. Did he see her as trouble? Jude should hate him because he was a patron of the club, but she could feel her nipples hardening from his gaze. Why initiate contact then? True, she wasn't rail-thin, but she wouldn't break him with her size. Or was he making fun? Everything was too confusing.

"Well, I sit on your lap and take some of my clothes off, Ramon." Jude's wobbly legs carried her across the small room to his position, and she dropped to her knees. "I'm supposed to dance and pleasure you, unless you have a better idea that's *legal*. I'm not one of the girls who say yes to anything. I have some limits." *Lots of limits.*

His dark eyes stole down her body with special attention to her average breasts. Were they too small? Was he thinking about the way her chest might bounce as they made love? Heat seared her to the core.

Jude leaned into him between his knees and kneaded the steaming bulge in his jeans with her hands. He was hard as steel. She gazed up at him, but saw only his poker face—no element of like or dislike, just blank and unnerving.

She wanted to look sexy or simmering, but felt ridiculous. Her confidence waned. What was he thinking? Did he like this? Did he want more…or maybe for her to stop? She needed to know if she was even on the right track or wasting their time. Then she wondered about the biggest question. Why her?

He commanded her onto his lap with a pat on his firm thigh. "Come here. I've seen you up on that lonely stage, Jude. Now I want to experience you in private."

His eyes seemed to soften with intent as he searched her face. She felt naked yet confident. He wasn't laughing yet. What about when he discovered how little she knew about satisfying a man? He'd laugh and run away.

Jude braced her hands on the arms of the chair and forced herself to slide onto his lap. Her heart slammed violently in her chest. "Please call me Jude." She straddled his muscle-corded legs and gripped the chair for support. "Is this better?"

Ramon's hands hovered over her forearms. He licked his lips, teasing her to partake. "Can I touch you, Jude?" His breathing sped up. Earnest sincerity graced his face.

The question and his subsequent actions knocked her totally off-kilter. *Can you touch me? Can you touch me? Everywhere and in every way, you can touch me. I'll die if you don't...* She had no idea where the thoughts came from, but she didn't discourage them. For once she wanted to run into a man's arms with abandon—this man's. "Yes, Ramon."

Shivers ran from her hairline to her toes. His brown eyes drew her in and his sincere smile gave her courage. A little bit of courage, anyway...

Her body moved on instinct—thrilling, sensual instinct.

Jude shifted to give him better access to the shirt. She wished it was his shirt with his scent. Her breath hitched as his long fingers grazed her breasts. He skimmed her sensitive skin with the gentlest of caresses, bringing a whimper from low in her throat. It was like he was being intentionally careful—like he knew about her past. Her skin flushed. She'd been waiting for ages for this moment.

His eyes lit up. "God, I want to see you, babe. You're beautiful."

Ramon's heavy-lidded eyes crinkled at the corners and a slight bit of colour darkened his stubble-covered cheeks. He leant forward and rubbed his nose against her neck, teasing her skin and giving her a glimpse of his scent—woodsy and masculine.

Jude allowed herself a tiny moan.

"Yes, sweet girl. Tell me this is real." Ramon grasped her hips to rub his cock with her crotch. They moved together slowly, building hungry need. He sighed and nipped her neck.

Although she wore the bra, she felt completely exposed in his arms and like she could get lost there forever...

Ramon felt like he had come home. The desire to reveal his real name, to hear *Drew* slide off her tongue, made it hard to concentrate. Ramon Decker existed on paper and nowhere else. Damn the operation. He slid open the sides of her shirt, revealing two perfect breasts with taut, rosy pink nipples, and couldn't help but grin. Jude shied away and wriggled. Worry clouded her eyes. Did she think he wasn't good enough? No, he saw her apprehension—she was waiting for him to put her down or cast her aside because of her job or her looks. Ramon wanted to beat the hell out of the bastard who had made her believe lies like that.

"Everything about you is an asset. Never hide your assets." He needed to touch her body and explore. She was every bit as he'd imagined, maybe more. Flames of desire licked his body from within.

The shirt fell away and pooled at his feet. She wasn't naked, but he thought she should be. Naked and in his bed... He groaned and she shivered. He looked into her ice-blue eyes and opened his mouth to ask if he could touch her face, but instead he paused. Images of forever flashed through his mind. Jude saw through to his soul.

Ramon cupped her face gently in his hands and blurted, "Jude Nelson, you deserve better than a dive like this." He wanted to sound alluring—instead the words sounded fatherly and tight.

She shrank back from his touch almost as if he'd slapped her. She looked small and helpless, all because of his unintended coarseness. What was running through her mind? Probably the urge to escape the man who was acting like all the rest.

The need to protect her surged through his system. She had to be at least six or seven years younger than his thirty-six. The hurt in her eyes made her seem tough, but she couldn't hide the vulnerability. None of that changed the fact that he wanted her—not as Judy, but as Jude, the real woman. What if he could unleash her wild side? Jude slid off his lap and covered her breasts. "Your time is up. I need to go." Her face was ashen and she averted her eyes. Ramon noticed her chest quake.

His chances to gain her confidence dwindled. He held out his hand. "Jude, stay. I asked for this because I wanted you and no one else." He didn't want to let her go. She fascinated him and he felt drawn to her body. Ramon shoved the distracting thoughts aside, praying she wouldn't leave.

Her eyes darted from his to the floor. He could get lost in her eyes, no matter what storms brewed there. He wondered what was going through her gorgeous head. Would she bolt or call the bouncer? He didn't want her to throw him out.

"I'll never force you to do something you don't want to do and that's a promise, Jude."

Instead of running, she sat back down on his lap, straddling his heat. Her fingers laced with his. "You've got me, Ramon," she whispered, "for now."

Ramon grinned but felt a strange sensation beneath his ribs. He didn't want her for only right now. He wanted her for... No, he couldn't say it. He didn't want to ruin it like everything else, especially not with the severity of the undercover operation gaining steam. "Then I'll count the minutes until I can kiss you, sweet girl."

Her eyes widened and her lips parted. There was a definite catch in her breath before she leaned into him. He loved that he could make her melt so easily and wondered if she would for anyone. Her eyes closed and a tiny sigh escaped her luscious lips. "Kiss me, Ramon."

Ramon cupped her face in his hands and brought her lips to his. She had to know how he needed her — wanted her. It was a quick kiss, but it seared his lips instantaneously. The combination of lipstick, mouthwash and Jude nearly knocked him out. Her tongue grazed his lips and he sucked her into his mouth — tasting...enjoying her.

Jude paused one more moment. He could tell she liked it...a lot. She touched his chest with shaking fingers. A groan erupted from her throat and she rubbed against him. Heat radiated from her pussy on to his lap.

"Woman, you're perfect for me," he murmured.

"I'm...just me." Jude fumbled for words and piqued his interest. Ramon assumed she didn't hear words like that very often. Most women pushed the envelope — Jude exhibited clumsy inexperience. Even with the sexy bra and thick makeup, he could see the little girl inside. This was a woman who had been forced to make hard decisions in order to survive. She had class.

"I want to take you home. I need to." Ramon rubbed her ass—so smooth against his skin and just the right size for his hands. Soft, supple and perfect.

"You can't take me home. I'm not supposed to date clients."

He brushed his thumb over her supple bottom lip. "Ah, but you're wrong. I'm the new bouncer."

She chewed the corner of her mouth. "I shouldn't."

Ramon could see the wheels turning in her mind. She probably didn't believe him. He wanted to give her satisfaction for a long time. "Why? Our working together is the perfect time to get to know each other."

Jude shook her head, making her breasts jiggle. "My common sense is telling me your idea isn't a good one. I need to go."

A lock of silky mahogany hair dipped in front of her clear blue eyes, making his cock strain against his jeans. The feeling in his heart went beyond superficial lust. The horny but protective cop in Ramon took over. He brushed the lock of hair from her face, relishing the texture in his fingers. She was cautious...good girl. "Ross did my background check. I'm clean."

She cocked her head. "Why me? I'm the total opposite of most of the other dancers." There was a hint of unabashed curiosity in her voice that sent a jolt through his body. Ah, the reckless streak again—no experience, but willing to try with the right man. "I'm a sucker for blue eyes and long dark hair." He cupped her chin. "I find sincerity and honesty a turn-on as well. Give me a chance. I'll prove I'm worth your hassle." God knew she was worth far more than a moment's hesitation.

The corner of her mouth crooked up and her eyes softened as she searched his face. "I'm not easy, you know."

Ramon chuckled. "Good. I like a girl who'll give me a run for my money."

All night long.

Chapter Three

Jude bit her lip and toyed with the hem of his shirt. She rubbed the pads of her fingers on his palm. Ramon grinned. One touch, one taste of this woman wouldn't be enough. Hell, one night with her wouldn't suffice. And, for a man who didn't get caught up on women, especially those he hardly knew, he was in dangerous waters. But he'd be damned if he didn't like it. He liked her too much for his own good. She'd seeped into his veins and made him want to be a better cop...to end the drug ring, and give her a future. *Oh man.*

"What would you like me to do?"

He brushed a feather-soft kiss over her lips. Another taste only whetted his appetite for her. He nibbled on her jaw, drawing deep from her natural perfume, a mix of rose and woman. "Ah, sweet girl, just let me touch you."

She threaded her fingers through his hair. "Touching isn't what I'm here for, but I can't think of a better idea."

Ramon cupped her jaw. "I want to touch you everywhere and thirty minutes isn't enough." Her eyes widened. Maybe that reminder hadn't been his best bet... "I wish I'd requested a private dance before now. You're addictive in all the right ways."

She opened her mouth to answer him, but a knock on the door interrupted their conversation. Jude sprang into action, picking up her shirt and turning towards the door. Tiny poked his head around the steel barrier. "Didn't mean to interrupt, but we need you out on the main floor, Ramon. Andre and Gavin can't restrain a drunk. Ready for action?"

Ramon grasped Jude's hand. He needed more time. "In a moment," he growled.

"Always a girl or a fix." Tiny chuckled and stepped away from the door. His mirth disappeared in an instant. "Two minutes or I fire your ass. Both of you."

Jude clutched Ramon's shirt and pressed a kiss to his mouth. The flicker of her tongue on his lips branded him like a constant reminder of her interest and what they shared. "You're dangerous, but he means every word," she said and slipped out.

Ramon leant back in his seat. He ran his fingers through his rumpled hair to digest the situation. *Dangerous.* This could be the start of something spectacular. His heart screamed yes, but the upcoming sting operation pummelled his brain. She came with strings—girls like Jude wanted to get married and have children. Would she want to stay with him? According to the file, Jude was an art student putting herself through college. He could only assume she coveted her independence. Was he man enough to be an equal in her life?

She had a power over him that scared and excited him at the same time. Somehow she'd touched him in places he'd long assumed were dead. He felt like she'd awakened the unfeeling zombie and reminded him that women could be soft. It was like she knew he needed time and a steady love—he needed a family of his own. No way he'd let her get away.

With kisses like that, I'll do my best to keep her.

Moments later, Ramon strolled out of the private room in search of Tiny's office. He ducked back through the main door to the bar room and glanced at the stage. A redhead with the tattoo of a fairy gracing her stomach writhed for the crowd.

"Like what you see?"

Ramon closed his eyes and gritted his teeth. Why did Carlie insist on connecting during this mission? He could do without her interference. "Not yet." He opened his eyes. "Can I help you?"

Carlie—as Goldie, in a gold bra and thong combo—grinned. "I'm Gold Dust Woman, but most people call me Goldie. Tiny told me to give you a tour." She held out her hand and linked fingers with his. "You look good with scruff," she murmured. "I like blonds. What's your name?"

Ramon directed his gaze over her head, back to the stage. Jude stepped into the spotlight. Tendrils of desire licked his body. The feeling of Jude in his arms stayed firm in his mind. No woman had ever sent such waves of heat through his system until Jude.

Goldie tugged the sleeve of his shirt. "If you work here, you can't gawk at the talent, but you can get your kicks for free."

Kicks for free? Ramon frowned. Trust Goldie to expect more than any man would give. He turned his attention to the stage. Damn, he could stare at Jude forever. He nudged Goldie to the side of the room and groaned to cover the lust in his voice. "You asked a question. Let's talk while we walk."

Goldie huffed and pointed to a hallway with a bright cobalt-blue door. "That's the dressing room. The bouncers aren't allowed in unless a catfight breaks out or he's invited." She wriggled her eyebrows. "Want to investigate with me? We have showers and everything."

Through his peripheral vision, Ramon noticed Jude on stage. She clutched the bright white dress shirt to her breast and bent to pick up the money at her feet. A smiled tugged the corner of his mouth. He wanted to run his fingers through the curls cascading around her shoulders.

Goldie stepped into his line of vision and glared. "You never gave me your name! Don't make me hurt you."

Ramon groaned. Why ruin a perfectly good show with insipid chatter? "Ramon Decker. Now where's Tiny's office?"

She tossed a lock of bleached blonde hair over her shoulder and span on her stiletto heel. "This way."

Ramon followed behind. When Goldie stopped short, he ploughed into the back of her. "What the…?"

Goldie turned and wrapped her arms around his neck. "I see you like Judy. Well, we can't let you waste your good looks on one woman. I want my turn with you." She stood on her tiptoes and forced a kiss to his lips. "I'm not finished with you."

Ramon grasped her shoulders and put distance between them. Goldie tasted of cigarettes and beer, not his favourite combination. She smelled of smoke and perspiration. He gagged. The song blaring over the stereo system segued into a frantic metal song. He glanced at the stage. This time, a svelte woman with hair the colour of coal sashayed around the silver pole and removed a jewel-encrusted bustier from her enhanced breasts

Tiny appeared from behind another patron. "Enjoying the show, Ramon?"

Goldie cackled and hooked her fingers into his belt loops. "See? Judy Blue Eyes doesn't even know you're not interested. I can make you so interested."

Tiny slapped Goldie's ass. "Run along. You're the next dancer up."

Ramon rubbed his forehead with the pads of his fingers and sighed as she scurried away.

"Yeah, she'll try your patience if you don't speak blunt with her." Tiny lit his cigar and blew smoke rings over his shoulder. "Not many men would walk away from Goldie in favour of Judy. You're wise and foolish at the same time. Every man on staff has tapped Goldie at one time or another, but no one's gotten close to Judy. Are you game?"

Ramon nipped back a smile. Jude wasn't like the other girls. Cautious, high standards, and sexy as hell. All reasons to like her...a lot. "I'm game. Now where's the fight?"

* * * *

Jude got through the rest of the night, but it seemed to take forever. Naughty thoughts took hold in her mind and even naughtier glances at Ramon heated her body. She replayed the feeling of his kiss on her lips. The texture of his tongue and the scent of his earthy cologne sent shivers up and down her spine.

The sexual element of her dances intensified as she thought about Ramon. She plucked her breasts and rubbed her inner thighs. He nodded his silent approval. So why did she feel the need to guard herself? She nibbled the tip of her index finger and dragged it across her bottom lip. Because something about him niggled her, like he wasn't being completely straight with her. She stole another glance at him. *Nah...*

Her facial expression brightened and her actions became more believable. It was like she had a glow that had never been there before. Her tips reflected her new outlook. So did the rude comments thrown her way.

"Babe, you can shake that ass for me at home tonight!"

"Come over and share your sugar with me — I've got a salty surprise for you!"

"Touch those tits for me!"

Jude shook off her disgust. She felt degraded and wanted to run. At the same time, a rush of excitement coursed through her veins. Was that what Ramon wanted from her? Maybe being the object of his desire wasn't so bad. At least it was attention for a throwaway kid like her. Any recognition meant everything.

At the end of the night, when she was towelling the sweat and smoke off her body, Jude ran into Renee. "Don't get attached to him. Men like that seem great, but they have a nasty aftertaste." It was the closest thing to friendly advice Renee had ever given anyone. "Tiny's got him working here. You know how I feel about in-house romances."

Jude nodded. "I know. Egos get in the way of the job and good people leave you in the cold. Don't obey Tiny's rule unless you want your heart broken... I know. I don't want to go through that kind of pain."

"It's too late," Renee said sadly. "You're into him as much as he's into you."

Jude shook off the feeling and packed her bag. She walked out of the dressing room to locate Ross, her favourite bouncer. "Hiya, hunk!" Ross was the muscular, balding father figure she'd always wanted. Her own father had never paid her any attention. She had been an unwanted surprise, and he'd blamed her for the condom breaking. Her mother had never cared enough to protect her youngest child from the man's angry, abusive wrath. Not Ross. Honest and protective to a fault, she knew he was her strongest ally.

"I'd rather keep you safe than see you get hurt and know I did nothing. What do you think of our new guy? Is he up to snuff?"

The cool September air raised goosebumps on her skin, chilling her to the bone almost immediately because Ross wasn't much of a windshield. She wished she'd remembered a coat or at least a sweatshirt. "He's a good man. He didn't try to paw me when Tiny gave him free rein. I find it a bit suspicious and flattering at the same time. Do you think he's Silver Steel material?" She shivered in her teal Silver Steel T-shirt and thin blue jeans. At least she'd had the foresight to remember to wear a bra. "He was supposed to walk me to my car, but I doubt he's got time. Goldie threw herself at him, not that I'm surprised. She throws herself at everyone." Her inexpensive plastic watch said seven after two. Her heart sank with each passing minute. Foolish. Ramon lied to get what he wanted and disappeared when it mattered most. "I'll bet he forgot."

"He'll come." Ross put his arm around her. "He's different and he's honourable." Jude grinned. Ross had never been fond of any of her proposed dates. "Tiny's got him doing paperwork right now. Drive up to the door and I'll send him your way."

"I can do that." Jude unlocked the door to her rusty red Neon. Not much of a car, but it got her where she needed to go. "Better yet, tell him I went home and will see him tomorrow. I have a meeting with my professor about my exhibition and need my sleep. He shouldn't care."

Ross nodded. "Goodnight, Jude."

Jude stepped on the gas and headed across town to her apartment building. Her eyelids drooped despite the urge to return to the club and hunt down Ramon. She parked the car, locked the doors, and stepped into the empty elevator. "I'll dream about him tonight and decide if he's worth the trouble tomorrow."

* * * *

Saturday night, Jude danced to the same songs and charged her moves with a sensuality she directed at Ramon. He stood guard by the main doors and winked once. She imagined his hands caressing her body and his kisses on her lips. When she walked off the stage after her last turn, she shook with pent-up energy.

Andie grabbed her arm. "Going to hunt him down?"

Jude bit her bottom lip and glanced at her friend. "Should I? I want to, but something's holding me back. He's been here lots of times before Tiny hired him, but still."

Andie peered beyond the curtain to the crowd. "Looking at him, I hear you. He's got an air of conquering hero to him, like he's never come across someone he can't bend to his wishes." She wrapped her arm around Jude. "But I also watched him stare at you. That man's in lust. He grabbed a man by the scruff of his neck and escorted him out of the club without taking his eyes off you."

Jude scrunched her nose, but couldn't hold back the smile. "Yeah?"

Andie let the curtain fall back into place. "He's on break. Why don't you go out there and plop down on his lap? I'll bet he'd love it. Wear the red tank top with the slit."

A fresh rush of excitement hurtled through Jude's veins. She raced to her makeup table. When she caught sight of her reflection in the mirror, she paused. Pink tinged her cheeks. A sparkle shone in her eyes. She puckered her lips and fluffed the curls in the clip holding her hair away from her face.

"He sees the beauty you hide and I'm sure he digs it." Andie dropped the top on the table. "Go get your man."

Jude struggled into the tight garment and adjusted her bust. She took a deep breath and fanned her face. "Do I look nervous? I'm scared to death."

Andie winked and Jude strolled out of the dressing room. She needed this. Needed a stable relationship in her life and to be cared about. Sex would be the icing on the cake. Maybe he'd be the one guy she wouldn't have to play up to and could be herself with. Then again, maybe he'd be the one to cut her down. The handsome ones always had the barbs that cut the deepest. As much as she wanted to fall into his arms and explore his body, she hesitated. *My heart won't be involved.*

Before she even reached the table, Ramon stuck his arm out. Jude swatted his hand away. "Expecting someone?"

He span in the seat and tugged her onto his lap as he wrapped her up in an embrace. "Only you, sweet girl."

Her heart fluttered and she tamped down the good feeling. "Really?" Her voice squeaked. "I'm far from sweet."

Ramon smiled, his white teeth glimmering. The walls around her heart melted a bit. "When you're with me, I feel like I can conquer the world." He trailed his fingers over her spine, sending shivers through her body. "I want to ask you a question. What are your plans after work?"

She dug her nails into his shoulders for balance. "It's Saturday and we aren't open tomorrow, so I planned to go back to my apartment, sleep and catch up on my homework."

He slid his hands up her sides to cup her face. His thumbs skimmed over her jaw, crumbling her defences a bit more. "Come to breakfast with me. I know a quiet little diner in Crawford where we can talk over bacon and eggs. Then I'll leave you to your studies."

Although *yes* teetered on her tongue, she forced herself to decline. "I can't." *Because I might find that I like you too much to walk away later.*

He knotted his brows and chuckled. "You're going to make this hard on me."

The corners of her mouth kinked. "If I make it easy, then what's the point?"

"My sweet girl's a smart girl." He tucked a lock of hair behind her ear. "I like that."

A voice over his mic system interrupted further argument. "Decker, break's over. We need you at the entrance."

He sighed and squeezed her thigh. "It's one twenty-four. Think it over. I'll meet you at the dressing room door and you can tell me then. I have to go help remove someone."

Jude slid off his lap and stood. She made a rash decision she hoped she wouldn't regret. "Okay, I'll come. But let me drop my car off at my apartment first."

Ramon threaded his fingers in her hair and brought her lips to his in a searing kiss. "Your wish is my command, sweet girl."

* * * *

An hour later, Ramon drained his bottle of beer. He sat with Andre—a hulking, raven-haired man of over six feet in height. A perky blonde strode out of the dressing room door and winked at Andre.

Ramon cocked a brow. "Is she your girl?"

Andre leant forward and curled his fingers into a fist. "You double dippin'?"

Ramon peeled the label from the amber bottle. "Nope. I got my sights set on Jude. I just thought I'd make conversation."

The man relaxed and sat back in his seat. He crossed his ankles and arms at the same time. "Me and Andie had a thing a while back, but right now she's seein' some lowlife named Tobey. She knows I keep an eye on her for her safety. I married a former dancer, Jill McQueen. She went by Rhiannon when she still worked."

"So things are working out for you?"

Andre shrugged. "I couldn't stand seeing the drunks drooling after her, so we decided that I'd be the only one to see her goodies. She wanted to quit anyway.

Got tired of the late nights and she wanted a family. Tiny paid for the honeymoon."

Corey emerged from behind the dressing room door. "Andre!" His smile dropped and he slipped a handful of condoms into his snug jeans pocket. "Decker."

"Put that shit away," Andre growled. "We know what you're doing."

Ramon cocked a brow, half expecting an explanation.

"Not in front of the newbie," Corey snapped. "And Judy Blue left through the side door. She went home. Wasn't that into you."

Ramon sprang from his seat and spoke past the lump in his throat. Maybe expecting her to be his informant wasn't such a great plan. "No problem. I wasn't waiting for her anyway." Like hell. He nodded at Andre and Corey. "See you Tuesday?"

Andre dipped his head and stood. "Six o'clock on Tuesday."

Corey grunted.

Ramon tossed the bottle into the nearby waste barrel and strode into the foyer.

"Wait up!"

He turned on his heel to see Jude running across the tiled floor. The red and grey flannel shirt slipped off her shoulder, revealing the strap of her crimson tank top and creamy skin. Her cheeks flushed a soft pink. She panted and stopped a foot away from him. "I thought you wanted to see me."

"I did." He grabbed her hand and linked his fingers with hers. "I just fell for some bad information. May I walk you to your car?"

She lowered her gaze. "I insist. Saturday nights seem to bring out the worst in people."

Ramon inhaled the sweet scent of her body spray—roses or something floral. His heart thumped against his chest. Being with Jude seemed like the most logical thing in the world. "Where do you live, sweet girl?"

Jude stopped by the rear bumper of a worn red Neon sedan. She cocked her head. "With you."

"Huh?"

"The Sanborn apartment building, where you live. Tiny expects all his employees to live there. Didn't he ask you to move in there yet? And don't call me sweet girl."

Her sass piqued his interest. "I'm sorry...Jude. I signed my lease a month ago." She furrowed her brows, so he fumbled for a lie. "I needed a cheap place to stay after I left my last place. Ross suggested the Sanborn—guess that's why. As for the nickname, you'll have to settle for 'sweet girl'. I save that name for the special women in my life."

Jude unlocked the door and tossed her bag on the passenger seat. "Only call me that if you mean it... Being one of your many women isn't my idea of great. So, why'd you leave?"

"I left for lots of reasons I'd rather not bore you with." Ramon held his breath. She was asking questions he couldn't answer, not just yet. He held her door open and leant forward to kiss her cheek. "But Jude? You are a babe and a sweet girl."

Ten minutes later he parked next to her in the Sanborn lot. Jude scampered to the right side of the car and climbed in. "I figured you for a truck, Ramon."

Ramon reached across the console and laced his fingers with hers. God help him, he needed to touch her. "I had a maroon S-10 extended cab, but it wasted too much gasoline."

Although she didn't pull away from him, the twenty-minute drive to the diner passed in silence. Ramon caressed the skin on the top of her hand, memorising the feel of her softness. He held the door for her as they entered the restaurant. Jude murmured a thank you and averted her gaze. Didn't men treat her with respect? Probably not, with the calibre of men at the club. He'd fix that.

An elderly waitress with two yellow pencils stuck in her frosted blue hair escorted them to a table. "You two are the earliest risers of the morning."

In accordance with his better judgement, Ramon sat opposite Jude. "Order whatever you like, sweet girl."

Moments later, the waitress disappeared with their requests and left them alone. Ramon took Jude's hand in his. She tensed then relaxed. "What's wrong, Jude?"

She shrugged. "This is my first sort-of date in over two years. When guys find out what I do for a living, they expect horizontal meetings and I don't play that way."

His heart wrenched. "Then let me make it up to you."

A smile curled the corner of her mouth and slowly lit up her face. "How do you suggest you do that?"

"A kiss here and a caress there, with kind words mixed in."

"That's corny, but sweet." She crinkled her paper placemat. "So did you notice—?"

Ramon kissed her hand, enamoured with her honesty. "Your beauty? Your charm? Or do you mean the fact that I'm drawn to you? You make me a better man when you're with me." He had to stop the syrupy words from slipping from his tongue before she questioned his integrity.

She laughed and stared at her lap. "You get cornier by the minute, but no." Jude brushed a lock of hair behind her ear. "I mean the cameras in the apartments. Tiny thinks we don't know, but they're everywhere. It's like he doesn't trust us and has to see everything we do."

His ire rose. Trust? *See everything*? The fucking pervert. Before Ramon could question Jude further, the waitress returned with their food. She left again without a word. Ramon toyed with his scrambled eggs. "I'm corny because I care." He dropped his fork. "Jude, what doesn't he trust you to do or not do?"

She munched a piece of crispy bacon and shrugged. "Talk to cops."

He swallowed hard. "Why?"

Jude stabbed a chunk of hash browns. "He's sure they'll find out that the girls go above and beyond the call of duty." She tapped the plate. "And then there's the condom packs that aren't really condoms. Some are, but some…"

"What are they?" Like he didn't have a pretty good idea…

She lowered her voice and shrank back in her seat. Her brow furrowed. "Drugs. Cocaine and heroin. You've been given some to sell, haven't you?"

"He gave me some to peddle. I haven't had time." He poked the sausage link. "I've kept an eye on you. You don't sell. How do you keep yourself clean?"

"I keep my mouth shut, but see… You work there, so I figured you knew." She froze. Her eyes widened and her cheeks paled. "Why do you look like you didn't know?"

He flicked his fingers to swat away her fears. "I'm supposed to test you. Nothing big, promise." He smiled, hoping to reassure her.

Jude dropped her fork and rubbed her temple. She inched to the edge of the booth seat, fumbling for her purse. "I need to go. Breakfast was great, but I need to go."

Ramon stood and touched her arm. Jude paused. Her shoulders slumped. "Honey, you didn't tell me anything I didn't already know. It's fine."

She covered her face in her hands. "You don't understand. He's got eyes everywhere. He probably knows we're talking. It's what happened to Slade and Astra. And I like you. I don't want to find you..." She trailed off and her eyes widened. "Never mind."

Ramon wrapped his arms around her. Her sobs wracked her body and made him tremble. The operation at the club went deeper than the force even figured. Randy—as Slade—must've got too close. What had Randy known? What had he seen? Hell, what had she seen?

"Take me home, Ramon."

Ramon kissed her temple. He needed to talk to Wallace, but, damn, he didn't want to let her go. "Yes, babe. I'll take you home. I'm sorry I pushed." He flipped a handful of bills onto the table and led her out of the diner. "Let's get you home where you feel safe."

* * * *

Forty-five minutes later, Ramon strolled alone, not into the Sanborn, but into the foyer of the MacAdam Grande Hotel in Carrington Falls. The urge to beat the hell out of the drug lord weighed heavily in Ramon's mind. Who gave Tiny the right to live out his voyeuristic tendencies with unsuspecting women? He grinned at the redhead behind the counter. "Hello, lovely. I need the room key for five-oh-six."

She handed him the key card with a piece of paper wrapped around it.

He nodded and sauntered away. Around the corner, he unfolded the note. *Use the motorcycle when you leave. Balthazar put a tracker on the Nissan.* Damn it. Balthazar knew where they'd gone. Probably heard the conversation through some sort of spy system. Ramon balled his fists. Jude shouldn't have to work for the bastard. She didn't deserve to live in fear. She'd earned the right to have a normal life. Tiny's behaviour merited nothing less than a six by nine cell…and yet right now Ramon worked for him.

Ramon continued to the meeting room. He knocked and inserted the key card. Time to tell his fellow officers what he knew.

Chapter Four

Four hours later, Ramon stopped outside Jude's door. His heart slammed triple time within his chest. After the briefing with Mateo and the verbal sparring with Wallace, Ramon had doubted his day could get worse — until he'd found all the miniature cameras in his apartment and cursed the fact that he hadn't checked for them earlier. Never gave it a thought. Who wanted to see every little thing the employees did on their own time? His thoughts wandered to Jude. Would she give him the time of day? He prayed she'd listen to him, if for nothing more than how to destroy the cameras.

Emotions he wasn't used to and fears he didn't need collided in his brain. If there was something going down, he didn't want Jude in the middle of it. He wanted to protect and cherish her. Hell, he wanted to lo —

No, better not go there. Whenever he loved, he got heartbreak in the deal for free — in spades.

Jude answered on the second knock. Puffy red ringed her eyes and her hair fell around her face in tangled curls, like she'd been crying before she'd fallen asleep. The enormous stock car racing fan shirt hung on her small frame. He fought the urge to yank her into his arms and kiss away her tears.

"Hi, sweet girl." He peeked over her shoulder. Sure enough, the same art decorated her wall with the same faux-gilt frames. The dome light on the ceiling bore the exact same bulbous knob as the one in his apartment. "Can we talk? I forced myself on you and I wanted to apologise."

"Trust you to be noble. Bastard," she mumbled and tugged him close. "He knows." She turned her head to the side and shouted. "I can't be with a man who doesn't respect me."

Ramon cupped her jaw and pressed kisses to her cheeks. "Then be with the man whose heart is in your hands. I respect everything about you." Twin sensations of delight and desire washed over him. He respected everything about her. And, in the short period of time since he'd met her, she meant more to him than any other woman. He nibbled her earlobe. "How?"

She whimpered and nuzzled his neck. "A phone call. He told me where we went. With details." She raised her head and spoke in a strong voice. "Get the hell out of my apartment."

He shook his head and crushed her in his grasp. "You're mine." Her lips parted and he kissed away her protestations. "Pack an overnight bag. We'll go somewhere and talk." Ramon wound his fingers in her hair and winked. "You're going to my apartment—like it or lump it." Unless a better option presented itself.

Jude turned on her heel and stormed into the bedroom. Ramon followed hot on her heels and punched the frame, right in the camera's tiny lens. She dressed, but, to add to the farce, he hefted the bag over his shoulder.

"Let's go. I'm not waiting." He wrapped his fingers around her arm and led her out of the apartment. "This way." Ramon scrambled down the back staircase to the parking lot and motioned for Jude to get into his car.

"Are you sure he won't see us? I'm scared." She frowned. "What happened to the Nissan? What's going on?"

Ramon engaged the engine. "The distributor cap on the Nissan blew sky high, so I borrowed my buddy Phil's car. Pain in the ass, but it happens."

"Do you think he bought it?" Jude dropped her head to his shoulder. "I trust you. I don't know why, but I do."

Ramon drove four blocks and stopped in a fast food parking lot. Things were happening too fast for his comfort and yet a part of him didn't care. Rescuing her, being her white knight, appealed to him all the way to his core. "I want to take you away from here for a while so you can unwind. I promise to be a gentleman. Do you trust me enough to take a chance?"

Jude nodded.

Ramon peeled out of the parking lot and drove another eleven blocks to Drew's apartment. He stopped in front of his storage garage. "We'll ride in style." He grinned and backed his Harley out onto the gravel. "I'll tie your bag down on the back."

She stood silently as her belongings became one with the machine. He removed his worn black leather jacket, draped it over her shoulders, and gave her a squeeze. "I think you need this more than I do." *You look better too...*

She slid her arms through the warm sleeves then caught him in an embrace. "Thank you."

Jude mounted the bike and settled against him. Ramon ignored the silly grin tugging the corners of his mouth. She felt too damn right to be wrong.

He pulled away from the kerb and headed west out of Carrington Falls. Thoughts raced through his mind as they sped down the main drag. He wanted to hurry home and get down to business. Then again, he also wanted to cruise the strip all night showing off his lady love.

Was she his lady love? He shook his head. This was too powerful, so it had to be the real thing. How could it be love? Everything seemed unreal except the grip of her arms around his midsection.

He desired to kiss every part of her body until she begged him to stop—to experience her warmth and make her come. Would she allow it? He wanted to ride around all night and hold her tight, so she'd never let go…

The thought of having her around long-term really tripped him up. It was a gut response and he couldn't tamp it down or push it aside. Where was this coming from? It sounded like he truly cared. Ramon had to stop—he couldn't give her a solid future. He'd been down that road and it only led to pain. He was a cop, not Superman, and he wasn't in love with a woman whose heart he had to break.

He breathed in the night air. The scent of her natural perfume mixed with rose petals twirled in the breeze. It was intoxicating. Too intoxicating. Ideas of forever coiled around his brain, muddling his thoughts. Jude had blind faith in him—she believed he would take care of and protect her. She didn't trust the cop because she didn't know the cop. She trusted Ramon. Once she fell in love, she'd give her heart, forever.

He'd sure as hell like to try to give her a future in his arms.

Jude rubbed her cheek on the back of his neck. The gesture sent shockwaves of desire ricocheting through his body. He could almost taste the softness of her skin against his and the heat pouring from the special place between her legs. What went through her mind? Did she fantasise about him? Did she ache for him?

He hit a slight ridge in the pavement and Jude's hands shifted to Ramon's waist. She gripped tighter. Blood and excitement rushed through his body at warp speed. A blush grew on his cheeks. He liked her attention. Her hand gravitated to the bulge in his jeans. A shiver ran the length of his spine. Bold — he liked her bold.

Oh my...my...

Ramon shifted in the seat to allow her better access. Delicious pleasure rocked his body. Heat surged to his cock as she stroked and caressed him. He'd finish before they got off the bike at this rate, but he didn't want her to stop. He released one hand from the handlebars and grasped hers in sign of ownership, but that wasn't what he desired. Theirs would be a mutually respecting passion. No one compared to Jude.

* * * *

An hour later, Ramon rolled down a stony lane. Fields of green and yellow surrounded them like a live, warm blanket. A white farmhouse welcomed from the east and a collection of brick-red barns stood to the west. The sweet smell of clover and pungent country air wafted through the breeze. Jude took a deep breath, savouring her surroundings.

"This place is beautiful, Ramon." She gasped when he brought the bike to a stop. Her chin rested on his shoulder. "Why leave here to live in that shitty apartment building?"

Ramon kissed her hand and helped her off the chopper. "I spent my summers and a couple of periods of self-confinement here." He wrapped an arm around her shoulders.

Jude span around twice, trying to soak in the sights. Everywhere she looked was an opportunity for a painting or photograph. "This is the kind of place to raise children," she murmured and shielded her eyes from the sun. He grinned at her and nodded in agreement.

"Drew?"

They turned in the direction of the bold baritone voice. "Uncle Elmer, what's the trouble?" Ramon laughed heartily and stuck out his hand.

The older gentleman took his hand and shook it vigorously. "Thought you weren't coming around these parts no more." Elmer grinned at Jude. "I see why now. Good job."

Drew nodded. "This is Jude Nelson. Jude, this is my uncle, Elmer Alwyn."

"I thought you said your name was Ramon?" What wasn't he telling her?

He shrugged. "I'll explain later."

Jude nibbled her bottom lip, but she couldn't stop the smile. Elmer looked like an older version of Ramon or Drew or whatever his name was. Elmer's temples were greyed and his step was a little slow, but otherwise he looked fit enough to run the farm single-handedly. Both men shared the same mischievous eyes.

"I hate to interrupt your visit." Elmer turned to Ramon. "But we got a cattle problem. I can't seem to get Ray on the phone and Logan's not answering over at the Malone place."

Ramon looked puzzled, making Jude snicker. "Cattle problem? Gramma Edna's only got two cows," he replied. "How did they get through the fence? Ray and I fixed it last summer good and tight."

Elmer nodded and folded his arms. "Max got spooked and Matilda followed him across the road. I need you to help me wrangle them back before the Kincaids find out."

Jude tried desperately to cover her giggles. Between the tough manly stance they shared and the slight scent of manure, it was all too much. The grumpy neighbours and pernickety farm animals only added to the scene.

Jude couldn't hold back her laughter any longer. "Max and Matilda?"

"We personalise our livestock." Ramon raked his fingers through his dishevelled hair. "Mind going in to meet Gramma Edna? I know she'll be dying to see you. She won't bite hard, I promise. I'll be in as soon as we get them back into the barn. Okay?"

Ramon looked confident but sceptical—like he knew she'd be all right but regretted leaving her alone. Jude knew he wished he could be with her, but the need to help his family outweighed the obligation to her. She'd be fine—always was…eventually.

Jude winked at Elmer and narrowed her eyes at Drew. "Unhook the bag and I'll brave the storm." She gave in to her giggles. "But you'd better tell me the truth soon." The idea of Ramon wrestling with a cow gave her hysterics.

Moments later, Ramon and Elmer disappeared behind the barn. Jude headed towards the house. She could do this—this was Ramon's family. *A bit early to meet his family.* Did he consider their relationship something that could become deeper? Did she want an actual love relationship with him? She raked her fingers through her hair. His grandmother was probably a very nice woman. Then why was she so scared? Possibly because he'd left her alone to get acquainted, that's why. Everything had happened too fast.

Jude paused a moment and fought the urge to throw up. She and Ramon weren't really involved, but there was no escaping now. *Breathe…just breathe.*

When Jude got to the porch, she saw a lone, fragile-looking woman sitting on the swing. Jude shored up her courage. Frail? *No sweat, I can do this. I'm scared to death, but I've handled violent drunks, so handling her can't be that hard.* "Hello," she called.

"Hello." Gramma Alwyn patted the seat. "Sit down. I want to get to know you."

Edna Alwyn appeared to be about seventy years old, maybe a tad older. Despite her advanced age, she was full of spunk and animation—nothing frail about the woman. Her silver hair rustled slightly in the breeze and her brown eyes sparkled with unasked questions.

Jude crept over, took a seat on the swing, and decided to grasp the bull by the horns. She twisted to look the woman in the eyes. "What do you want to know?"

"I can see exactly why Drew picked you." Edna patted Jude's knee. "You look a lot like his mother, but not completely."

Jude smiled weakly and looked at the ground. "Drew doesn't talk about his family. In fact, he's never mentioned them. He told me his name is Ramon."

"Oh, that's his middle name." Edna stared out at the cornfield. Her thin hands knotted together as she spoke. "He's very quiet when he wants to be."

"Why is he quiet? What happened?"

Edna grinned and waved her hand. "Let me show you a couple of pictures. I think that may answer your question." She led Jude into the cavernous farmhouse. "By the way, you can call me Gramma or Edna. I don't care which. Ramon calls me Gramma unless he's in trouble — then I'm 'the grouch that hollered at him'."

Jude stifled a chuckle. Edna stood maybe an inch shorter than Jude, but she exuded a force, like she could put Ramon in his place with only a verbal command.

Jude followed Edna into the sitting room. The scent of mothballs and perfume permeated the space. Photographs of Ramon's family lined the walls. Among them were his graduation photo, a wedding photo, and one of him with two younger women that looked an awful lot like him.

Jude studied the pictures and winced at the ones she didn't like. Seeing other women who were no longer in his life made her wonder why they had ever walked away. She supposed the others had never seen the diamond buried in his rough exterior. Or was she missing something?

"That's Nat, his first wife." Edna pointed to the wedding photo. "She was a nice thing, but too picky. She wanted Drew...I mean...Ramon to save her from a nasty situation. When he wanted her compassion in return, she turned her nose up at him. Stupid girl."

"What happened?" Jude dug her nails into her arms. Seeing Ramon with another woman was strangely uncomfortable, yet comforting. Without the others as dead-ends, she and Ramon might never have found each other. Still…he'd had a wife? He didn't seem like the type to settle down. Why would a life with her be any different?

But Ramon was the only man she couldn't pass up. She'd enjoy the good time while she had it.

"He's gone a lot… You know, on the job," Edna said. "She expected him home every night. When she didn't get what she wanted, she walked out. Her father never liked Ramon, so immediately they got together and rushed into marriage. It was a mistake, but he had to learn somehow."

"Who are they?" Jude pointed to the women in the third shot. Based on their clothing, the photo appeared to be about ten years old. With less stress in his life and fewer creases on his face, the man in the photograph looked rather angelic, especially with brown hair. Somehow, Jude favoured the weathered look, but with his natural hair colour. "Are they part of his harem?" It was a lousy attempt at humour that fell flat.

"His sisters, Chloe and Erin."

Jude's eyes widened and her throat constricted. *Sisters?* That was definitely something she hadn't seen coming. Her voice cracked. "He's got sisters?"

Edna shook her head. "He'll never talk about them directly. He's older by four years. Chloe's thirty-two and Erin's about your age, I'd guess."

Jude looked away to compose her thoughts. Edna had to regard her as a dunce. Either that or the woman must wonder what honest couple forgets to mention family members. Jude ran a shaky hand through her hair. "I see."

Edna turned to Jude. "Their father, my son, was a drunk—a nasty son of a bitch, if you ask me. He beat the tar out of those kids and Ramon took the brunt to keep the girls safe. He's a born protector. And, to this day, neither of them has ever thanked him. They think like Natalie did. He had his use and, when it was up, they were gone too. It's sad, but that's life. Unforgivable really. They haven't spoken to him in at least ten years."

"What about his mother?" Jude searched the wall for a family photo. No wonder he'd stayed silent. Why remember someone who chose to erase you from their life? "Where's she? I don't see her."

Jude's stomach clenched and her palms became clammy. Hiding her growing discomfort had become a daunting task. Did she resemble a woman who wasn't good enough for the memory wall?

"You won't find her up there," Edna replied. "Carol walked out right after Erin was born. She left raising the children up to Robert—who, in turn, left it up to an eight-year-old Ramon."

Jude sighed and tried to clear her mind. She didn't need to know the entire background on Ramon Decker, yet Edna seemed to want to spill every little detail.

Jude turned to see Ramon out on the front lawn leading a brown and white mottled cow back to the barn. She pointed to the animal and tried to change the subject. "Who's that?"

"Matilda," Edna replied with a giggle. "Max is all black."

Not far behind Matilda, Elmer led a reluctant Max back to the barn. The poor cow mooed in protest.

"Max is stubborn, just like Ramon," Edna said and wrapped an arm around Jude. "He's complex, but not impossible to decipher. You'll need to be his strength and his sensitivity. I know he loves you very much."

Jude turned to look at the older woman. *Love*? He'd never said a word about love in their whole three days together. "Oh, really? How do you know?"

"Because he brought you here. No other girls have cut my mustard—not even Natalie. He's particular and deeply in love." With that, Edna walked out of the room.

Jude stared at the wedding photo. It seemed so stiff and fake. She wondered if there was a different story hiding just below the surface. At the same time, Jude looked around wondering where Edna had disappeared to. An edgy feeling crept up her spine. Maybe she didn't belong here and the whole scene was nothing more than lip service.

Before she could worry further, Edna returned with a worn piece of paper in her hand. "You see this girl?"

Jude glanced at the picture and then at Edna Alwyn. She inspected the image. Light hair hung in curls around a beaming, much younger face that could only be Edna in her prime. A flowing skirt hugged her slim figure while the cinched gingham bodice accentuated her full bust. Sugar and spice sparkled in her eyes and brightened her mischievous smile. No wonder Ramon's grandfather had married her—she was gorgeous.

"That was me in my heyday with Ramon's granddad. Alice Stockman had legs to die for, but I had Jonas. He was just like Ramon. He fought so hard to be tough, but all he ever wanted to do was protect the people and things he loved. He saved me from a charging bull when we were kids. He knocked me out in the process, but I fell in love with him anyway. The lump on the head had nothing to do with it."

"That's sweet." Jude grinned. Edna was the grandparent she'd always dreamt of.

"Ramon saved you."

Jude twisted her fingers together. "Maybe."

The entry door banged shut. Edna opened her mouth as if to speak but never uttered a sound. Ramon rounded the corner. His boots sounded heavy on the hardwood floors.

"Gramma? What are you telling her?"

Jude's wide-eyed expression melted his anger. Well, he wasn't really angry...just frustrated. There were things Ramon had wanted to keep under wraps until he'd found the right time to explain. Like revealing his real name. He should've suspected Elmer and Gramma would say when he brought Jude to the farm.

"I told her the truth." Edna gestured to the photo wall. "We looked at pictures and talked about you. I told her that you got the chicken pox at three years old and ran around stark naked because we couldn't keep the medicine on you any other way."

"You did not. Besides, I was four when I got the pox." Ramon crossed the room and slung his arm around Jude's shoulders. He smiled quietly and sighed slowly to mask his feelings. It felt like all the air had rushed out of his chest. "She told you everything, didn't she?"

Jude snuggled into his embrace. "She told me enough."

"Even who the neighbours are?"

"I never said a thing about living next to celebrities. But I will." Edna pointed out of the picture window. "Next door is that actor, Logan Malone. Behind us is

Ray Russell. He's got a band. Nice folks—quiet but nice. Cass Malone sends over proof books before they come out and brings Julian by to play. He's a doll baby—so chubby and giggly. Logan and Ray help out when Elmer and I need a hand. I couldn't ask for better neighbours."

"Well, now you know the whole story." Ramon kissed the side of her head and stared at his family in the photographs. As much as he tried to stifle the urge, his body stiffened. Memories flooded his mind and hardened his heart. There wasn't enough anger in the world to make up for his past, but holding Jude made bearing it easier. And she had no idea.

Edna fluttered her hands in the air. "I have to talk to Elmer and start dinner. Feel free to show her the sights. I assume you'll stay in your room tonight?"

He nodded.

"Goodnight then, for now." With that, his grandmother scurried from the room.

"Well?"

Ramon swallowed hard. "Well, what, sweet girl? This is my home and she's my grandmother."

Jude turned and cocked her head. "Is Ramon your middle name?"

Ramon continued to look at the wall. "Uh-huh." He'd rot in hell for that lie. Or would he lose Jude? He wasn't sure and didn't want to find out. A slow burn of anger and frustration simmered in his belly. He wanted to leave, just to walk away, and forget the drug bust. That wasn't likely now, though. "So, what did she say, Jude? I can take it."

Jude squeezed his hand. "Short version—this is Nat. She's selfish and left you." Jude then pointed to the photo of his siblings. "These girls are your sisters—ungrateful brats, so I was told, but still family. And this is your father, the alcoholic. Your mother isn't pictured because she's gone."

Ramon swallowed hard. Jude knew Drew's story.

"That's pretty much it," he snapped.

Jude chewed the corner of her mouth. "I'm not sure why your Gramma told me all those things, but it makes me understand you a little better."

The muscles in his jaw began to clench and unclench. Had he finally found the woman who could help him move forward? He'd wanted her to know the truth, just not like this.

"I want to show you around." Ramon wrapped his free arm around her shoulders. "You ever watched the sunset behind a pond?"

Jude pulled the jacket tighter around her body as they walked outside behind the house. "I'd like to."

She was so damn beautiful he could hardly stand it. He couldn't tell if she was cold or scared.

He longed to reach in and know what she thought. He felt her bristle slightly when they reached the grey wooden bench next to the pond. He wanted her to feel many things for him, but fear wasn't on his list. Far from it. Why was she scared? What wasn't she telling him? He'd give his life to keep her safe.

"Talk to me, sweet girl." He sat down and propped his arms over the back of the bench, giving her freedom to move. "Tell me what's on your mind." His feet shuffled silently on the tufts of bottle-green grass. Ramon didn't know how he could expect her to open up about the goings on at the club. He just wanted to help. It wasn't the cop speaking. He was starting to care even more than he could begin to comprehend.

Her eyes met his. She had cool, consuming blue eyes that reminded him of serene pools. He wanted to tell her everything—his name, his occupation, his fear of snakes…

His desire to stretch her over the seat of his Harley and fuck her until she screamed his name three times over…

Jude chewed her bottom lip and picked at the cuff of his jacket. Her nails scarred the butter-soft surface. "Do you think I'm a prostitute because of where I work?" Her voice was small and choked. Her hands shook. "I know the rumours and I know what the other girls do. Tell me the truth."

Ramon felt like she'd stabbed him in the heart. She'd cut him right to the bone with her blunt question. The orange glow of the setting sun silhouetted her body.

"I know you want sex." She swayed back and forth, twisting her fingers. "I want to know how you feel and what you're planning to do. I don't see why you're trying to make me feel like I belong. I'm nobody."

"We're here for you to rest." He patted his thigh with his right hand and held his left hand open. "I wanted to see you because I like you. I never expected anything else. If we have a relationship, then wonderful—if not, no problem. I refuse to push you into doing anything you're unsure of. And no, you're not a nobody."

No problem? No pushing? Leaving Jude alone would be a huge problem. One taste just wasn't enough. To win her trust—and, ultimately, her heart—Ramon would wait forever. "Why don't we talk? Just talk…about whatever's on your mind."

Worry etched Jude's beautiful face, but he could see her body relax a bit more. Was she considering his suggestion or devising a plan to escape? "Promise?"

Ramon nodded "Cross my heart."

Jude dropped onto the bench next to him. Her arms stayed tight against her body while her eyes scoped out the scene, never totally allowing herself a chance to breathe. "What do you want to know?"

Ramon propped one foot on his knee and toyed with his jeans cuff. "Why are you afraid of Tiny?"

"Because he's not afraid to hurt people for sport. Slade wasn't like the other guys. I think he was a cop. He carried himself differently, with more...stature. He cared about the girls and made a point to talk to all of us. When Tiny found out about him and Astra, he had a meltdown. We never saw Astra or Slade after that. I never heard what happened, other than they ran off to Vegas together. But... I doubt it." She stared at the glittering water. Ripples shimmered light across her face. "I know—you probably think I should have a better job. I've heard the argument before."

Ramon dropped his chin to his chest. More confirmation concerning Randy. *Fuck*. "I haven't heard your rationale. Tell me."

She chuckled. "I'm not the prettiest girl there. Goldie gets that award. I'm not the most coordinated either. That's all Andie. So, for me, it all boils down to studio time."

He hooked his fingers under her chin and closed the gap between them. "Look at me, sweet girl...please? Studio time for what?"

Her gaze vacillated between his eyes and his lips. "I'm studying to be an artist. I have about two months to go and I'll have my degree in studio art—unless I have to miss a lot of classes. Finding the time some weeks, when Tiny's being an asshole, is tough and I hate it." She worried her bottom lip. "The best time to get into the studio is the early morning. No one's around. Most students wait until late at night. I work the opposite so I can have time to myself, usually."

Ramon slid his hand along her jaw, rubbing his thumb over the bone. "You could do more..." She looked away. He inched closer to her, cupping the back of her head. "But you're doing what you need to in order to survive. No one can take that away from you."

Her lips parted and her eyes widened. Ramon leant forward, not about to miss the opportunity. He swallowed her whimper. She wound her arms around his neck. He twined his fingers in her hair, savouring the silky texture.

Jude groaned. She straddled his lap and snuggled closer to him. "You love to surprise me, don't you?"

"Among other things." Ramon wrapped his arm around her waist. Blood pounded in his ears and surged to his groin. This woman would be the death of him and he welcomed the challenge. He wanted to taste her, drown in her. He needed to re-learn every inch of her.

Jude grasped his shoulders and hovered centimetres from his lips. "Take me in the house."

Ramon nodded. "I want to make love to you, sweet girl. I want to feel you surrounding me." She shifted to stand and he held her fast. "But I refuse to take advantage of you."

She backed away a few more inches. Sadness clouded her blue eyes. "You won't be."

He pressed a kiss to her swollen lips. "You're scared and don't trust me enough. First, I'm going to show you what it's like to be home."

Chapter Five

A single table lamp illuminated the enormous room, giving it a cosy, intimate glow. A handful of photos and a couple of concert announcement prints hung on the bland sand-coloured walls, with a garish beer clock adding interest above the bay window. Otherwise, the bedroom was rather barren. He watched her and wondered what she thought. Was she displeased? He'd change anything to make her happy.

Ramon stopped at the foot of the king-sized bed. He could imagine her living with him and being completely happy. She looked perfect in his home. The farmhouse could be theirs...

He shook off the feeling of ease. She wasn't his...yet. She might never be. He tried not to expect what couldn't be, but the thought lingered. What if she was what he wanted—his missing piece? His gaze followed her. His entire being sought her touch.

Jude sat down on the edge of the bed. She glanced around the room. Her smile remained thin.

Ramon crossed the short distance, sat down and pulled her onto his lap. "Tell me what's on your mind, sweet girl." He cupped her cheek. Her light perfume continued to drive his senses wild.

Tell me you love me...

Whoa! Where'd that come from? He bit back the goofy smile curling his lips.

She squirmed to get comfortable. His erection pressed against her backside with delicious tension. He had to get himself under control—no need to spook her further. Her lips parted and her eyes closed, sending a fresh wave of desire crashing through his body. If she kept that up, he'd be a goner.

Strike that—he was already on the ragged edge and in danger of going over.

Ramon tugged her close and brushed his lips to hers. He could feel her shiver again, this time with delight. Her sensuous moves made his craving surge. He pushed the kiss further, not wanting to break their connection. His tongue brushed past her lips and slid against her teeth, mimicking the rhythm of lovemaking.

At first, Jude fought him, but gradually opened. He swallowed her moan—proud that he could still produce such a reaction in a woman. They needed to go further—he wanted all of her.

Not yet.

As if she'd been shocked, she pulled back. "I thought we were going home. You said you wanted to wait."

"This is my home. Where I really live and where Tiny isn't watching every last thing I do." Ramon smiled and chuckled. "Do you know how sexy you are?"

She shook her head. "You confuse me."

"I can't keep my hands to myself, but I promised to be a gentleman." He brushed a lock of her hair from her eyes. His fingers trailed down the side of her face. She shivered. "You're all I think about, sweet girl. How I want to kiss away your fears and protect you against the bastard that wants to control our lives. In a short time, you've become very important to me."

Jude thumped his arm. "You say that to all the girls."

Ramon wrapped his arms around her and kissed her temple. "Just the adorable ones. I don't bring just anyone to meet my gramma."

The blush ran from her collar to her hairline. "So, what do we do now?"

"We'll find some cheesy movie on the television and get crumbs all over the bed. I promise."

She cocked her head. "Yeah?"

He cupped her jaw again and feathered kisses from her earlobe to her lips. "You can use my chest as a pillow. I won't even kick you out for snoring."

Jude burst out laughing. "Deal."

"One condition."

"What's that?"

Ramon covered his eyes with his hand and peeked through his fingers. "You'll hold me during the scary parts. I'm a wuss in badass clothing."

She bit her bottom lip, but giggles spilled forth. "I doubt that, but I could probably offer you some assistance."

Ramon joined in her laughter and touched his forehead to hers. "My sweet girl."

* * * *

Two hours and one bag of ranch chips later, Ramon flicked the television off. Jude sighed and snuggled closer to him. His gaze roamed along her prone body. She had every right to be asleep—she worked a crazy schedule in order to pay her bills and, with Tiny's intrusions, worried herself into a frazzle.

He, on the other hand, was wide awake, although it was nearly two in the morning. He brushed the crumbs off his shirt and yanked the blanket from the end of the bed over their bodies.

Jude snuggled closer to him as though they did so every night and rested her head on his shoulder. She sighed and went still. His heart did flip-flops—could she love him? He stared at the stark white ceiling trying to digest the events of the past three days.

She trusts me.

His heart screamed love and his head vehemently ignored it. This encounter was only supposed to be for her to recuperate after a long week. Then why did he want her to stick around in his life? Why take her to the farm and introduce her to his family?

Ramon stared at the ceiling. If Tiny kept tabs on her, then what did she have to hide? A niggling feeling in his gut wouldn't calm. Was he putting Jude in danger by choosing her? Was she in on the drug trade at the club? He doubted she sold the packets, but there was that inside chance she could be lying.

Her hair tickled his jaw. Deep down in his gut, he knew she wasn't in on the trade. Her involvement shouldn't matter, but it did. Damn it. He cared about her. He cared too damn much. She made him laugh, think and burn with a white-hot passion he'd never known he possessed. And they hadn't even made love yet.

Ramon wrestled with his feelings and thought about his former lovers and ex-wife. With Nat it had been love, hadn't it? No, he'd wanted to be with her because she'd had the qualities of a stable mother. Theirs had been more of a tepid friendship than a sizzling love affair. Nat had felt sorry for him. She hadn't wanted him to be alone so she'd given in for that miserable year.

What about Carlie? He'd thought he'd loved her…but had he really? Not in the least. They couldn't stand to be in the same room together unless they were naked.

But Christ, this thing with Jude… It wasn't even supposed to happen. Getting involved with someone while undercover…

He was so fucked.

Ramon tucked his free arm behind his head then kissed the top of Jude's head. Her silky hair tickled his cheek once again and her light scent danced in his brain. She draped her jean-clad leg across his. Her breath was light and warm against his skin. His heart leapt. Even in sleep, she had the ability to turn him inside out. And they had yet to make love… Damn, thinking about sex with Jude gave him a boner.

What made her 'the one'?

He wanted to adore and protect Jude. He craved her love in return. How could he show her how desperately he needed her to need him? Jude was the type of woman he could be with forever. She was his ideal vision of the mother of his children.

Would she agree?

Because of the early hour and his lack of sleep, irrational thoughts entered his head and wreaked havoc with his common sense. What if she only wanted him as a means to escape the wrath of Tiny? What if she figured out he wasn't just a bouncer? She wouldn't use him to escape punishment, would she? *What if…?*

He looked at the clock.

Two-nineteen in the morning.

Ramon closed his sleepy eyes involuntarily and pushed the silly, irrational thoughts from his mind. He'd deal with those things in the morning. For now, he'd revel in his precious time with his Jude.

* * * *

Jude woke the next morning with a start. She rubbed her eyes. Where the heck was she? Korn poster on the wall. A large black bureau sporting a small, flat-screen television. The tan walls felt more like a day at the beach, rather than a bedroom. Like an embrace.

Like *his* embrace…

"Good morning, sweet girl."

She turned her head. Ramon's voice slid over her soul, smooth and easy. "Hi." She peeked under the comforter. "We're still dressed."

Ramon propped himself up on his elbow. A wicked grin turned the corners of his mouth. A sprinkling of hair darkened his jaw. "You're surprised?"

She kissed his chin. "Pleasantly surprised to find there are still a handful of gentlemen roaming the earth. What time is it?"

"Ten. I let you sleep. When's your first class?"

She swiped a hand over her face. "Five past eleven and I need to change. I won't be intruding on your gramma, will I?"

"She lives on the first floor. Her knees can't handle the steps." He pressed his lips to her forehead. "I'll be downstairs waiting."

Jude hurried through a shower and wound her hair into a clip. The faded jeans and T-shirt would have to do. She gathered her makeup and notebook into her messenger bag. Ramon stood at the bottom of the stairs, a grin spread across his face.

"What?"

"You." He threaded his fingers with hers. "I like the fresh look. Reminds me how young you are."

"Is that bad?"

"Not in the least."

Thankful the college was on the close side of town, Ramon pulled to a stop in front of the Vestige Arts and Theatre Building. "How long?"

"Three hours."

"I'll be back when you're done." He smoothed his hand over her cheek. "We'll do supper before you have to go in."

"You got it." Jude kissed him on the lips and climbed out of the car. She afforded him a wave and strode into class. For one of the first times in her life, the weight of her future wasn't so heavy. She didn't need a man to make her existence complete, but having his affection and protection gave her spirit wings.

As she unlocked her art locker, Professor Rosengarten ambled past. He gestured at the closet-sized changing room without a backward glance. "You have experience being nude, so it won't bother you. Step to it."

She frowned at his back. What a jerk!

Jude did as told because the class was a requisite, but his remark made her feel dirty and used. As she posed three feet in the air on the selection of rickety furniture in ridiculous positions, she took a deep breath. She wasn't opposed to being nude. Posing never bothered her, but the professor didn't need to be quite so blunt.

Jude ignored the questioning glances and snickers from her fellow students—she still had her pride. When school concluded in a couple of months, Jude would be free, unlike her peers. She held her head high, knowing she'd have done it on her own.

Being still gave her time to think about the previous weekend. Running off to the country was a bit out of character, but being in Ramon's arms—that was heaven. She glanced at the wall of windows. Cars rolled past in an endless cycle.

Ramon...

The thought of him warmed her body and sent a slow burn to the junction between her thighs. Her mind switched from ignoring the professor to her own private fantasy. It didn't matter if the class knew—she didn't care what they thought anymore. All she cared about was Ramon. Would he want to make love to her, even though she'd kept him at arm's length? She wanted to spend lots of alone time with him. What would sex with him be like?

Her mind wandered to a fantasy. She and Ramon were both in the drawing classroom, posing for a non-existent crowd. He wore only faded blue jeans and she was totally nude. Her skin sizzled with the imagined feel of his rough hands.

"*So this is how you spend your days?*" Ramon lowered himself onto the couch next to her and leaned in for a consuming, primal kiss. "*What's the fun of sitting still when you can be the action instead?*" His groin rubbed naughtily against her. The roughness of the zipper teased her smooth mound. God, she wanted his hands everywhere.

"Do you have a better idea?"

His eyes flickered sinfully. "*This.*" He nibbled her right nipple into a stiff peak. His left arm curled around to the back of her head. His touch was strong and demanding.

"And this..." He lowered his lips to hers. "Is this what you want, babe? I want to pleasure you."

"Ramon!"

He shoved his pants past his narrow hips and guided his cock into her sopping wet pussy.

"God, I want all of you inside me."

"Not yet."

Jude furrowed her brows. Not yet? No, she needed him right now.

"Miss Nelson, I'd like you to turn and lean on the back of the chair. Put your best face forward."

Jude blushed. *Oh.* She hadn't left drawing class. She nodded and complied with the professor's command. Had he caught on to her divided attention? Did he think she approved of his smart-ass remark? Not hardly.

"Drat," she muttered. Only a fantasy...

Jude's embarrassment evaporated when the professor added a partially nude male model to the mix. The model, who wore jeans, was a fellow art student named Aiden. He was handsome in his own right, with straw-coloured hair, hazel eyes and a crooked smile. A garish fraternity tattoo covered his right pectoral muscle. Good looking, but not what she wanted. He was nothing compared to the rush she got from the simple touch of Ramon's hand.

"Lie back against the couch so we can recreate an Odalisque." Jude shifted into position and threw her arm over her head. Good thing she'd remembered to shave.

"Now, Aiden, hold her as if she were the most prized possession you own."

Aiden bent over her and leaned in like he was about to kiss her. His right hand gripped her breast while he braced his left hand on the back of the couch. He anchored his right knee between her thighs with his left foot firmly on the floor. A sinister light lit his eyes and a wolfish grin curled his lips.

Jude clenched her jaw and averted her gaze.

"I never knew you were so hot," he whispered. "Stop covering yourself up in those stupid baggy clothes and be the sexy bitch you're meant to be."

Jude glared. "I'm not a piece of meat."

"Is this how you entertain men at the Silver Steel? Never saw you there, but I'm looking now"—he bobbed his brows—"for something special."

"No."

As if he couldn't hear the argument, Professor Rosengarten prattled on about the light on the planes of their bodies and how the models aroused each other. "Notice the electricity. Make sure you capture that in your work to make the audience feel the intimacy." He patted the couch above Jude's head. "Make the viewer feel as though he or she is part of the relationship."

Jude rolled her eyes. Maybe Aiden was horny—she wasn't excited in the least. She squeezed her eyes shut to prevent Aiden from getting the wrong idea. Her ideas settled on the thirty-six-year-old bouncer who owned her heart.

Jude wondered what Ramon was thinking or if he even missed her. Probably didn't care. She glanced out of the bank of windows by the door to the hallway. A set of chocolate brown eyes sparkled through the glass. *Ramon.*

Her breath caught in her throat. *He came.*

Ramon nodded. His smile brightened, showing off his white teeth.

Jude licked her dry lips. The man hadn't touched her, yet she felt closer to him than the man crouched over her. Maybe Ramon *was* the one for her.

* * * *

Ramon strolled past the rush of students leaving the classroom. A dark-haired girl with wire-rimmed glasses grabbed his sleeve. He turned.

She flipped long mahogany hair over her shoulder. "Class is over, but I could give you some private instruction. Interested?"

Shocked by her boldness, Ramon shoved his hands into his jacket pockets. "Thanks, but I'm meeting someone."

The girl shrugged. "Suit yourself."

He frowned and watched her disappear into the chaos of the hallway. Interesting.

"I see Tara spoke to you."

The smile tugged the corners of his mouth. "Jude." He ducked into the classroom.

Jude sat cross-legged on one of the benches. "She tells every man she'd like to 'tutor' them." Her chin rested on her curled fists. "I didn't think you'd show. Promises are easy to break when something better comes along."

"And miss out on spending time with you? There's no one better." He plopped down next to her. "Besides, I wanted to see what you do with your time."

"Other than dancing?"

He stroked her jaw. "Is modelling another one of your jobs?" Her eyes widened. Ramon backpedalled. "I mean... I don't know what I mean, but I didn't—"

Jude covered his mouth with her hand. "We take turns. It was my day to model."

He licked her fingers. She retreated. Ramon grasped her palm and kissed her knuckles. "You glow."

She cocked her head. Creases formed between her brows. "What?"

Ramon wrapped his arms around her. Her head tipped and their gazes met. "Sweet girl, I'd rather see you nude in private, but when you're posing you look natural. You are honest and happy when you're in your element."

Jude licked her bottom lip. She slid her arms around his shoulders, toying with the hair at the back of his neck. The combined actions turned his insides out. She inched close to him, her mouth a breath away from his. "I'm creating art. That's beautiful to me. I'm not a fan of the professor, but I've learned to deal."

Ramon crushed his mouth against hers, plundering her sweetness. Jude moaned. Her pussy rubbed against his leg. His heart beat a manic tattoo in his chest. When they parted, he gasped. "Beautiful suits you." He smoothed his hands over her back and butt, memorising her curves. "I like the look. Screw me for being biased."

Pink rushed into her cheeks. "How are you prejudiced, other than being slightly warped in your sense of beauty?"

"I like you…a lot."

Jude bobbed her head to move a lock of hair from her eyes. "Even with my unconventional job and less-than-stellar looks?"

Ramon pressed kisses to her cheeks, making his way to her ear. Her breath on his neck sent shivers along his spine. "I like you because you're Jude. The job has nothing to do with my feelings. And don't say you're not gorgeous. I will take you over my knee until your ass shines from my paddling."

She jerked out of his arms. Her hands covered the smile blossoming on her lips. "Really? Spanking?"

"Whatever works." He nodded at the benches. "Will you show me your work?"

Jude surged into his arms and rubbed her cheek on his chest. "Soon. I didn't get anything done today."

Ramon kissed the top of her head and stroked her back. "Then come home with me?"

Jude leant back a bit. "We live in the same building. You dropped me off." She cocked a brow. "Aren't you already going to take me home? Or are we taking another road trip?"

He cupped her chin. "Smart aleck. You knew what I meant."

She stuck her hands in his back pockets. "I'm keeping you on your toes."

Ramon held her close, leading her to his car. "You know how to take a sentimental moment and knock it on its ear."

"Then take me somewhere…anywhere with you."

"Yes." Ramon squeezed her thigh.

Ramon led her to his new ride. Jude stopped short and pointed at the rusty excuse for a car. "Let me guess. More car trouble? This thing doesn't look like it can make it five miles, let alone get us across town."

"She moves well for being a beater car." He opened the passenger door. "I didn't like the colour of the other car. I wanted to drive the Kia this time."

"You're a confusing man sometimes. Nobody goes through cars like you." She plopped down in the seat and gripped her bag tight.

"I'm fickle." Ramon grinned before he rounded the hood. He drove them across town, even though he'd rather have gone anywhere but the fleabag hotel. He had to keep up appearances.

He pulled into a parking space and killed the engine. "Ready to go inside or are you having second thoughts?"

"And lose the chance to see you naked for a change?" She opened her car door and slammed it shut. "No way, but slow down." Her footsteps slapped the concrete behind him. When he stopped to open the door, she wrapped her arms around his waist from behind. He tugged her into the open elevator car and turned around in her embrace.

"Okay, I'm a little...excited." She buried her face against his shoulder.

The bell for their floor pinged and the elevator opened. Ramon escorted her down the hallway and opened the door to his apartment. Instead of behaving like the confident woman he'd spent the weekend with, Jude ducked her head and crept past him.

"Sweets?" He closed the door, but kept it unlocked. "What, babe?" He led her to the couch and pulled her down onto his lap, giving her the advantage if she wanted to leave. "We can take things slow."

"I can't," she whispered.

"Can't?" Things didn't make sense. He'd tasted her skills, indulged in her sensual moves. She wasn't a...virgin?

Nah. She couldn't be.

"I've...never"—she waved her hands in front of her face—"done it."

A virgin. Holy fuck. Would he be man enough to satisfy her fantasy? His desire sped past hyper-drive into supersonic. Whatever was happening between them was so much more than lust or a need to notch his belt. He was falling for her...hard.

"I feel so stupid." Jude's fair complexion went bright pink. Her voice was a whisper. "I gotta go."

She attempted to get off his lap, but he caught her in his arms. He had to have her. No more panic, no more fear. He slid her back onto his lap and smoothed her hair away from her face. "You're a virgin." His heart pounded triple time. Even more reason to get her naked without a crowd watching. "I don't mind. Actually, I'm intrigued and honoured."

Her jaw dropped involuntarily. "You don't mind?"

His eyes searched hers. "I don't understand how you can get up there and dance for those fools, but if you've never had sex, I understand. Well... I don't really get it, but I don't care." Ramon kissed the tip of her nose. So it wasn't the smoothest explanation—chalk it up to testosterone logic. Desire coiled in his belly, making it hard to think straight.

"I haven't found anyone who I thought was decent enough to sleep with." Jude stared at her lap. "I've had boyfriends, but none were serious or treated me with any real respect."

He brushed his fingers along her jaw to bring her eyes to his. Intensity and raw desire filled her eyes. He needed to know where she stood. "What makes me so special? You could have your pick of willing men."

Jude brought her lips to his in a hungry, consuming kiss. "I don't get it myself, but you make me feel attractive and that's never happened before. I know you're holding something back from me, but I don't regret our time together."

Ramon returned her kiss with ferocity. Desirable, horny, needy, hot, spellbound...and on and on. It all described how she made him feel. But was she serious? No one had ever told her she was attractive? Were her previous dates blind? She was the most beautiful woman he'd ever seen, inside and out. The past and the undercover operation didn't matter—he wanted to be her future.

"I knew you were special from the moment I first saw you." He claimed her neck. Lord, he wanted her. "I don't regret a thing I've gone through with you."

Jude nodded and clutched his shirt. "I guess I need some instruction if this is supposed to go smoothly." Her voice was breathy, sensuous, and timid. "Please?"

"I'm a pretty good teacher." Ramon claimed her mouth once more. Virgin or not, he had to have her. The sooner, the better. Why? Because Jude was different. She made the blood course through his veins, as if she slammed every nerve ending in his body into overdrive without a second thought. Loving her was too easy and felt too right to be real. No way was he going to stop. The drug bust be damned for one night.

Jude curled into his body, pressing her soft curves into his chest. Her eyes drooped closed and she moaned. The sound of her excitement sent him over the edge, knowing he'd caused it.

Ramon smoothed his fingers over her breasts. Damn—she wore a bra. He longed to feel her bare nipples growing taut for his touch without hindrance. Next time. Her breath quickened and her hands shot up to clasp his. "Ramon!" His body wanted to rush her, but his heart made him take his time. For her, he'd progress as slowly as possible. Ramon kissed her hands and placed them at her sides. Her pleasure was of utmost importance. He could wait until later to sate himself. He kneaded her breasts. "You tell me how far we'll go."

She leant back just enough for him to push the jacket over her shoulders then pull her T-shirt over her head, tousling her hair. Her lacy white bra gave him a teasing peek at her breasts. The look drove Ramon wild. He brushed her hair away from her face and latched on to her collarbone. She answered him by tilting her head back to grant him better access.

"Take your shirt off," she commanded, seeming to forget herself. "I've seen you so many times, but I don't know what you look like. Show me."

Momentarily breaking their bond, Ramon ripped his T-shirt up over his head. She had deft fingers. His nipples pebbled under her touch.

The straps of her bra slipped off her shoulders as she bent to take one in her teeth.

A moan escaped Ramon's throat. Her passion-filled response both shocked and turned him on more. He hadn't thought this degree of lust was possible. He continued to brush her hair away from her face so he could watch her work. For a novice, she knew his body instinctively.

He couldn't keep his hands or mouth off her. He unhooked the catch on her bra in order to sample the rosy nipples he'd lusted after for the past few nights. The primal urge to conquer and own her threatened his common sense. She wasn't a slave available for purchase—she was a treasure. "So pink and perfect," he complimented in a gravelly voice. His hands tugged at the waistband of her jeans. He needed more of her...all of her. *Now.* "Babe, do you trust me?"

Jude's head bobbed up. A lock of hair obscured her flushed face. He sensed her hesitation.

"What?" Was she second-guessing?

"If you trust me, I'll leave you satisfied. Do you trust me?"

Jude hesitated and licked her lips before she unbuttoned her garments. She slid out of her pants and underwear in one swift motion. "I trust you completely."

Her unabashed faith dazed Ramon. He'd imagined her withdrawal because of his blunt question. When she didn't turn away from him, he wanted her even more. He could have everything.

Ramon caressed her bare ass. He swatted her playfully and enjoyed her yelp of pleasure. As she moved in to straddle his lap, the silky skin between her thighs captivated him. "You wax?" he blurted inadvertently. He felt like a clumsy teenager trying to get to first base with the homecoming queen. *Real suave*.

"I need to look smooth in a thong. There's nowhere to hide," she replied in a raspy voice. Jude's honesty continued to shock, rivet and rock him. She covered her stomach. "Well, I can't hide much."

Ramon bent to kiss her folds. "Do you know you're beautiful? And so honest."

Embarrassed, she turned her face from his. Ramon caressed a hand over her cheek to bring her eyes back to his. "Beautiful and perfect."

A tiny smile crossed her lips. Ramon nodded. *That's my sweet girl*.

"Do you like being kissed here?" He nudged her legs even farther apart and explored the undiscovered region of her folds and opening with his tongue. A shudder ran the length of his spine as Jude opened farther for him. He wanted to touch and pleasure her everywhere, loving her with his mouth. Slick and sweet. "What about here?"

Jude shifted and lifted her hips, giving him better access. "I've...never..." She gasped. Her nails scraped along his arms. Ramon teased her pussy and tasted her clit, basking in her excitement. He'd never taken much pleasure out of going down on a woman—he'd been too selfish...until he'd met Jude. She took him at face value.

His tongue darted around her throbbing wet clit, tormenting her to the brink of orgasm. To prepare her for sex, he slipped one finger into her sopping sheath. Jude bucked her hips and yelped. "Oh, God."

To heighten her climax, he added another finger. His tongue danced around her swollen clit while his fingers pumped into her folds, simulating intercourse.

Jude writhed and screamed his name.

Ramon couldn't get enough of the feeling of her muscles tightening around him. Wet, perfect and new—no question she really was a virgin.

"Come for me, sweet girl." He increased his intensity on her body. "I'm doing this all for your pleasure. Yes. Let it go."

She squealed. "I...oh!"

He knew she was holding back, afraid to give in to the orgasm. "I'll never hurt you. You're safe. Come for me," he said in a soothing voice. "I want to feel everything you have for me."

Her gaze connected with his. Her breathing hitched and her hips bucked off the sofa. Jude screamed. "Ramon!"

Ramon slowed his assault on her and eased up next to her sated body. Lord, he'd nearly come as he'd got her off. He pulled her into his arms and cradled her on his lap. What would it sound like to hear her call his real name? He wanted to know and soon. "Did I hurt you?"

Dazed, Jude barely shook her head in response. Ramon's mind wrapped around the fact that he was her first—she didn't know how to react and he wasn't sure what to think. Something deep inside him was pleased to claim her. "Talk to me, sweet girl."

She whimpered. "Wow. There's no words."

Ramon caressed her stomach. His fingers grazed over something smooth and foreign on her body. He glanced down her body to the barbell that glittered in the soft lamplight. The piercing itself didn't shock him—plenty of the other strippers had the same piercing. Why did she have one? Were there any others?

"Jude, when did you get the bellybutton piercing?"

She sighed and averted her eyes. "I did it to please a man." Her voice was hazy.

Ramon flicked the metal with his fingers. "Did it work?" He winced. Why was he suddenly afraid to find out?

Jude shook her head. "No. He said I looked slutty. I didn't want to do it, but he said that something daring would boost my self-esteem."

Ramon swallowed a bemused chuckle. The tiny thing looked daring and sexy to him. "A ring with a glittery flower or jewel would better fit your personality, from what I can tell. Why a barbell? "

Her eyes slowly met his. Sadness brewed, tugging at his heart. "I had a barbell with a flower on the bottom when I first got it done. He said it looked ridiculous. When he left me, I kept the piercing, but went with a plain barbell. It looked less obtrusive and reminded me that quick decisions make lasting impressions…or, in this case, holes. Plus, I equate barbells with strength—if that makes any sense."

He wanted to beat the man senseless for walking away from her. Then again, Ramon was secretly glad, or he'd have never had a chance with her. Before the night ended, he needed to make love to her.

"Have you showered since you left the college?"

Her eyes cleared and she covered her breasts. "What kind of post-almost-sex question is that?"

Okay, so he'd said the wrong thing. Uncertainty clouded her face and she shied away from him. He'd definitely screwed up. If there had been any trust before, he'd just killed it. She probably thought he was a hygiene freak.

"Trust me." Ramon kissed her shoulder and left a purplish mark. "I wasn't trying to run you off. I thought you might like to relax in a hot shower. With me."

Jude arched her brow but didn't back any further away. Instead she bit her lip, as if to consider his proposition. After a long moment, she nodded. "Okay."

Ramon allowed himself to breathe. An opening. Thank God for the opening. All he had to figure out was how to convince her to stay for more than one night. Talk about the impossible. He kissed her temple. "You'll love this."

Jude's eyes widened as she entered the bathroom. "Are you sure *this* will work?" She averted her gaze. "I'm not sk–"

Ramon brushed his fingers over her hand and felt her shiver. "Relax, sweet girl. You're beautiful." He wanted to pull her close and lick the sensitive spot on her shoulder where it connected to her neck. The faint scent of rose and aroused female tickled his nose.

Jude turned and nuzzled against his bare chest. Ramon groaned – he couldn't fathom how such a light caress could send his senses reeling. He shivered as she raked her fingers down his chest. Pinpricks of electricity heated his skin. The catch in her breath sounded promising. Did she like what she saw?

Ramon scooped her into an embrace. A small cry, like the coo of a dove, came from deep in her throat. He brushed his fingers along her smooth mound, the undersides of her breasts and lightly across her taut nipples. Jude shuddered, sensitive to his every caress.

"You're phenomenal." He took a puckered nipple in his mouth. "Sexy and primed."

Jude reached out to him then yanked her hand back.

"Explore away, babe." She could fondle whatever and wherever she wanted. He'd teach her anything she wanted to learn.

Ramon wanted to tell her that he craved her for the rest of his life. Hell, he'd never wanted a woman like he wanted her. She wasn't a one-nighter. She was a once-in-a-lifetime love — *his* lifetime love. Why was it so hard to admit?

Because, if Jude didn't feel the same, Ramon wouldn't survive the rejection.

Her eyes stayed glued to his chest as she spoke. "Have you ever made love in the shower?"

Jude's simple, innocent question caught Ramon off guard and he fumbled for an answer. He knew she was hip to his past — she had to be. Somehow, he didn't want to admit he'd had other lovers before her. He wanted her to be his first and last.

"I have, but I'd like to with you more than anything."

"Me, too."

Jude claimed his mouth under the spray of water. Things had definitely improved since that morning. For the first time in more years than she could count, she felt attractive. Ramon gave her hope that her future could be bright. And now the object of her obsession wanted to have sex with her. She wanted things to continue to get better, but the inevitable fall scared her shitless.

His calloused hands rubbed her ass. "Jude, I can't get enough of you."

Why did she feel so tempted to bury her face in his chest and simply breathe in his scent? Because she finally felt wanted and adored. Ramon lapped at her jaw and neck while whispering words of praise in her ear. She could stand this kind of treatment for a long time.

"I want to feel you all around me. Turn around." Ramon smoothed one soapy hand across her breasts and the other down between her thighs. He toyed with her clit, sending shards of lust through her body. "The first time will hurt, sweets. I can't change that."

"I know." Jude clenched her teeth—he had an immense cock. She glanced over her shoulder and nodded. "I want you to make love to me."

Ramon pushed his cock against the mouth of her pussy. *Oh God.* Was he going to fit? No turning back now. She flattened her hands on the chipped tile wall. Inch by inch, he entered her. She bit down on her bottom lip. The farther he went, the more it hurt, but it was pleasure-filled pain. Her breasts grew tight as they heaved and bounced with each thrust. The one and only time she'd attempted sex, the act had ended with pain and embarrassment.

"Touch yourself, babe. See how slick you are," he murmured. "You're doing everything right and making me crazy to fulfil your desires. The hurt will pass in a little bit."

Jude ignored the pain and ran her hand down next to his to fondle her slick folds. It felt crazy and out of sorts to touch herself, and even crazier to do it with a man, but Ramon wasn't just any man. He was the epitome of her naughtiest fantasies. The guy who made her body do things she'd never thought possible before. Could she feel this exhilarated with anyone else? She doubted it and didn't want to find out.

The burn between her legs shifted from pain to pleasure and each thrust made her feel more alive. Instead of fighting the feeling, she ground on him and met him action for action. Jude wondered what Ramon thought about as he impaled her on his surging cock. Did he enjoy her or was this just an act to fulfil a need?

She glanced over her shoulder again. His eyes rolled back and his teeth clenched together. Either he liked it, or his acting skills were impeccable. A low rumble came from his throat as he came. Jude bit her bottom lip and enjoyed the experience. Life had never been this consuming and raw.

"Come for me, Jude." His voice was a husky growl that sent a shiver of desire the length of her spine. "Let it go and ride me. Fuck, I'm coming."

Jude screamed in pleasure as the orgasm wracked her body. Hot seed coated her pussy and warmed her from within. Wet hair clung to the sides of her face in soggy tendrils. She pressed against the chill of the tiles and gasped for breath. Talk about an experience… Why had she waited so long to indulge in sex? She pushed the thought aside to deal with it later…much later.

Ramon braced his hands on the slippery shower wall on either side of her head. "Turn around, beautiful." The smouldering need burning in his eyes drove her senses wild. Jude had no idea what ran through his mind, other than fulfilment. Did he sense the same deep connection she knew existed between them?

With the flick of his wrist, Ramon turned off the water. Jude stepped out of the tub and used the closest towel to explore his body. She took in the ripples and valleys with intense interest. He was gorgeous, manly...and so out of her league. The connection was real, but his interest would wane. She wasn't sexy enough to hold his interest for long unless she proved him otherwise.

In a burst of moxie, she planted tasting wet kisses along his sternum to the slender patch of hair that led to his cock. Her tongue blazed a trail of passion along his taut abdominal muscles.

He moaned. "Oh, God, babe."

Heat seared within her body. She didn't want short term. As she'd done so many times on stage, she shifted her hips in time to the music in her head and dropped to her knees. "You've pleasured me twice — now it's my turn to love you."

Ramon twined his fingers in her hair, sending sparks straight to her toes. He groaned. "Yeah, babe."

Jude grasped his cock in one hand and kneaded his balls with the other. The springy curls and soft skin contrasted with the hard-as-steel rod saluting her. A bead of moisture glistened on the tip.

He gasped. "Babe, you're gonna make me come too soon."

His statement diverted her attention. Jude licked her lips. *Make him come? Good idea.* In one swift move, she took his cock in her hot wet mouth and simulated the sex they'd just had. Either she was a quick study, or he was a fantastic teacher. She guessed both.

Ramon's eyes rolled back in his head. A moan escaped his lips. His hands gripped her head, increasing her actions and making her wet once again. Jude hummed her approval and milked him to his second orgasm. She liked the taste of his salty offering mixed with soap and sweat from their bodies. She was living on the edge and loving every minute of it...and him. He tasted as good as he looked.

Ramon used one hand to brace himself against the sink. Jude inwardly grinned—she'd made his knees go weak. She released his semi-hard cock and licked her lips once more. She hadn't thought she had that kind of power. Maybe she did.

He scooped her into his arms. "I'm all for sexing in the shower, but I'm a traditional kind of guy. Why don't we try it in there?"

Jude giggled and nestled her face into his neck. Even after sex, he smelled wonderful and masculine. "By all means. Take me on your bed."

He became hard at her command. "Yes, sweet girl. We should do that." He dropped her feet to the ground. "After a nap. You've worn this old man out."

Jude snuggled into the blankets. Slumber filled her eyes and mind. "Sounds good," she mumbled.

Ramon laid her down on his massive queen-sized bed and curled up at her side under the sheets and thick comforter. "Was it all you expected?" He wrapped an arm possessively across her stomach. "I'm hoping I made it special."

I'm hoping I made you mine.

Jude turned to face Ramon. "Better than I could've ever expected," she murmured. "Now I see who I was waiting for... You." She finished her sentence, closed her eyes, and fell asleep.

Ramon baulked at her statement. Waiting for him? What was so special about him? Being a virgin, she could have had any man. He stared at the ceiling. Jude was more than one in a million. She understood him and didn't run from the dark parts of his soul. Well, she got Drew anyway. He rolled onto his side and nuzzled her hair. His eyelids drooped. Just a short nap...

* * * *

Ramon jerked. The screech of his cell phone ripped him from sleep. How long had he been out? He glanced at the clock. Only an hour had passed. Jude wriggled beside him, but didn't wake. Fine. He scrubbed a hand over his face and grabbed for his phone.

"Decker."

"You're late."

Ramon groaned. Corey. Trust the shit to give him shit. "It's six. I'm not due in until seven."

"Judy Blue's supposed to be on stage right now."

Fuck. "She'll be there."

"Just get her here within the hour. Or not. I'd love to fire you." Corey clicked off the line.

Ramon gritted his teeth. God damn it. There was only one way Corey and Tiny could have known about them being together at the same time. Did they have a tracker on her? A remote camera operation on her phone? *Fuck, fuck, fuck.*

Jude drew in a long breath and let it out slowly. "You look tense. Here." She crawled onto his hips and leant down. "Let me relax you."

He should be worried about her being sore. Should care about getting her to the club so she wouldn't have to deal with the wrath of Balthazar. But one touch of her slick heat against his cock threw his thoughts from the phone call. Screw the distractions. Time for Jude.

"Stand up, sweets."

Jude slithered off his lap and stood beside the bed. Anticipation sparkled in her eyes. "Now what?"

Ramon turned her around. "Hands on the mattress."

She glanced over her shoulder. "Like this?" She leaned over the edge of the bed and brought one leg up high, knee on the bed.

Ramon stepped up to her position. So much for being in control. "Where did you learn this?"

She reached around and guided his erection into her slippery pussy. He leaned into her and started to thrust. One taste of her wasn't enough. He wanted forever.

Jude ground her body into his and placed his hands on her breasts. "I'll die if you don't touch me."

Ramon obliged with a sexy growl. He wrapped one arm around her waist and used his other hand to pinch her swollen nipple. "We wouldn't want that."

Jude's eyes rolled back in her head. "If I wanted to learn things, I watched movies."

He slapped her butt with the flat of his hand, bringing a groan of pleasure from deep in her throat. "Smart-ass."

Jude arched her back and squealed with pleasure. "Yes," she said in a sensual groan. "Faster, Ramon."

He released her breast and gripped her hips to drive into her deeper. "You're such a hot, bad girl, sweets." She managed to push him to the ragged edge in less than a heartbeat. "I love bad girls."

She gripped the sheet and trembled. "Ramon! Don't stop. I'm coming."

His orgasm hit its peak with hers. He groaned, sated. "God, you're good." Ramon added a couple of extra thrusts once the orgasm had passed. He slid to her side and stroked her hair. "So good."

Jude took his arm and wrapped it around her body. "I can't move." She giggled. "But I like it."

"I don't think I can either." Ramon sighed and nibbled her ear. "Great sex will do that and I'd label this right at the top."

She wriggled onto her side to look him in the eye. "We need to get to work."

"I know." He growled. Damn it. "I'll take you in, little girl. I got a reminder call and you were supposed to be on stage an hour ago."

"Oh, Christ." Jude trembled and her eyes widened. "Just protect me. I like knowing you've got my back."

"Anything." He tucked her close to his side and stroked her hair again. *Just let me keep her safe and with me.*

Chapter Six

Jude tapped her fingers on the notebook in her lap and rolled her eyes. "AH four-thirteen."

Ramon cocked his head. She'd rarely used the phone in the three weeks they'd been together. "What are you—?"

She put her index finger to her lips. "AS four-forty-one."

Frowning, he peeked over her shoulder. Class catalogue? She'd not said a thing about taking more classes. If she had, how hadn't he noticed? He folded his arms and paced. Things at the club had hit a plateau, but that meant nothing. Drugs still swirled around the club and the girls continued to offer extra services. Tiny just observed it all.

If Tiny wanted to cause trouble, all he had to do was say the word and with the cameras everywhere... He glanced at the walls. A red light blinked in the vent above the door. Another fucking camera. Didn't Tiny have anything better to do than spy on his employees? For all Ramon knew, the tapes were ending up on the Internet.

He groaned and turned back to Jude. "What's up?"
Her shoulder edged upwards a fraction of an inch. "I missed too many class meetings this semester. I need to take one of my history classes and a studio class over if I don't manage a high enough grade. It sucks, but that's life."
Take them over again? That's life? He scoffed. He'd seen her work and knew she devoted herself to both her art and her job. *Well, hell.* "What can I do to help?"
"Besides make it so I can get more schooling done and work less?" She waved her hand. "I'm behind on one of my portraiture projects." Jude tipped her head. The corner of her mouth curled in a smile. "Can I use you?"
What did she have on her mind? "Didn't you use me three times already? Or was it four?" He chuckled. "Don't get me wrong. I loved every moment. Feel free to bend me to your will."
She licked her lips. "I want you to pose for me. I want to render you in charcoal."
Ramon grasped her hand and considered her words. A drawing of him. His body and her emotions captured on paper for anyone to see. Dangerous. Someone could recognise him if she used it for a class and yet he didn't mind. "How?"
"I'll use my charcoals and the sketch pad from class. You just have to sit or lie there." Jude slid from the bed. Her ass swayed as she crossed the room to retrieve her supplies. His mouth watered.
Ramon finger-combed his hair. "Okay." He slid from the bed to retrieve his boxer shorts. "How would you like me?"
Jude rushed forward and grabbed his hand. "Nude."
He cocked a brow. "Me?"
Jude nodded. "Are you scared?"

"Scared? Never." Ramon tossed the underwear across the room. "I'm game. Whatever you want, babe."

Pink flushed across her cheeks. "Really?" A smile started at the corner of her mouth and widened. Genuine. Sweet. God, he loved her natural beauty.

"How do you want me, babe? Stretched in front of you? Posed like I'm thinking hard? Or maybe I could re-enact that ridiculous pose the professor put you in."

Jude nibbled her fingernail. "I did have a pose sort of picked out."

Ramon slid his arms around her body. He kissed her until they both couldn't breathe. "Shape me. I'm yours."

She licked her bottom lip. "Recline on the bed like you're watching television." Jude wriggled from his embrace and arranged the pillows. "Don't look at me. Focus on the screen and hold still."

He stretched out across the mattress as she'd instructed. Jude sat in the armchair to his right. She closed her eyes and took a long breath. He couldn't smother the grin forming on his lips.

Each time her gaze strayed over his body, each time she studied him, the closer he felt to her. He shivered. It was like she saw through to his soul. Like she knew his secrets…and she didn't mind them. His connection to her became deeper, more intimate. Jude shared her body through their lovemaking. When she created art, she shared her entire being down to her soul. Damn, she was sexy when she worked.

A furrow crinkled between her brows as she concentrated. When she pushed her hair from her eyes, a bit of charcoal smeared across her forehead.

Blood surged through his system at warp speed. He'd thought he liked women who were elegant and refined. Why did that smear send his senses reeling? Because she was real, honest and unabashed. His admiration for Jude grew in proportion to his erection. He ran his tongue around his dry mouth. "Sweet girl, I need a break."

Jude tucked another lock of hair behind her ear, smearing charcoal across her cheek. "You can move. I'm done."

Ramon slid to the edge of the bed and stretched. "Show me. I want to see how you see me."

Jude blushed. The scarlet hue spread from her hairline to her breasts. She presented him with the sketch pad. "I see you like this."

Ramon snaked an arm around her waist and studied the drawing. She had indeed captured him. The control in his eyes, the hard line of his muscles, the birthmark on his thigh and the jagged scar on his chest. He chuckled. She had given him dark hair, despite the ridiculous streaks dyed into the brown. He looked tired yet strong, conflicted yet sure. She'd captured Ramon as his true self…as Drew.

"Sweet girl, it's amazing." He placed the pad on the dresser. "Come here."

Jude sat on his lap. Uncertainty clouded her blue eyes. Ramon cupped her face, rubbing his nose along her cheek. "I'll tell you what's just as amazing."

She sucked in a ragged breath. Her fingers wound through his hair. "What?"

"You."

She pulled away. Her lips parted on a small gasp. "Flatterer."

Ramon nipped her bottom lip. "You're mesmerising in the club, but you're sexier when you're creating."

Jude stared deep into his eyes. She opened and closed her mouth like she wasn't sure what to say.

"Talk to me, babe. I can see the wheels turning."

Her gaze never wavered. "I love you."

Shock thundered through his system. Sure, he'd wanted to hear those exact words from her from nearly the moment he'd met her. And now he couldn't take what she offered. She'd fallen in love with Ramon. Not Drew. *Fuck.* "Come again?"

She shook her head and wriggled in his grasp. "Nothing."

"Jude?"

"I need to go to the bathroom."

She scampered under his arm and disappeared behind the bathroom door. Ramon raked his fingers through his hair. She loved him. His heart clenched. She'd made love to him because she'd followed her emotions. How was he going to get her to love the man behind the disguise?

"Sweet girl, come out and talk to me."

Jude splashed water on her face once more to wash away the evidence of her disappointment. She'd told him she loved him and he'd acted like she hadn't said anything. Some men weren't good with emotions. Some men cared only about what they wanted. She couldn't read him. Did he care or not? Or was he the type of guy who wanted nothing more than an afternoon fuck?

She studied her reflection in the mirror. Red-rimmed blue eyes, flushed cheeks, mussed hair and a very nude body formed the image. A lump lodged in her throat. She looked easy, like a tramp. Nothing like a woman with morals and self-esteem. Did Ramon see her in the same light? She had bared not only her body to him, but also her soul. Tears burned behind her eyelids and she gulped air. Time to walk out with dignity.

Jude twisted the knob and opened the door. Ramon stood on the other side with one hand propped on his hip and the other hand rubbing over his face. "Honey, I—"

She placed her index finger over his mouth. "Ramon, don't." Her heart ripped in half within her chest as she held firm to her pride. Jude scooted past him and grabbed her clothes from the floor. "I need to go."

Ramon touched her shoulder. "Why?"

Jude tugged her jeans past her hips and yanked her T-shirt over her head. "I need air." She edged past him and strode to the door.

"Jude?"

She froze.

"Honey, I'm not the type of man who can tell you he loves you. I'm not sure what love is. I refuse to sell you a line of bullshit." *Until I'm sure I can give you what you need.*

"I know." With that reply, she walked stiff-shouldered into the hallway and down the corridor to the stairwell. As her bare feet moved over the worn carpet, Jude replayed her time with Ramon in her head. Tears burned her cheeks as they slid from her eyes. How could she have been so foolish as to think love would come after a few weeks? It wasn't like she knew his life story—only bits and pieces. Why did her heart feel raw and exposed? Because she cared about the man. She loved him.

She burst through the door to her floor. A voice in the back of her mind nagged at her. Was he worth it? Was he really the man who deserved her heart and what was left of her virginity? True, she'd made a failed attempt at sex once with Neil McDaniel, but with Ramon it had been a transcending experience. He made her feel sexy, wanted and cherished. Why did those emotions seem so foolhardy now?

Because she loved him and always would. *I'd relive the whole relationship again in a heartbeat.*

Jude stood before her door and rifled through her pockets. Damn, no keys. She puffed out a long breath and dropped her chin to her chest. *He's got my keys and my purse.* She touched the peeling brass knob. The door creaked open and her blood ran cold. She dragged air into her lungs in an attempt to calm her frayed nerves.

Jude gave the door a shove, yet stayed in the hallway. "Hello?" Maybe she'd left the door ajar when she'd gone out in such a hurry the other day? She shook her head. No. Locking her door was second nature.

She scrubbed a shaky hand over her mouth and ventured a foot into the apartment. She flicked on the overhead light. The curtains to the lone window fluttered in the stiff breeze. Glass shards and the torn remnants of her clothing lay scattered all over the floor. Drawings flopped in between the piles of strewn pencils and drawing pads. Her blood thumped in her ears. She was a smart woman, but suddenly she felt like a fool. Being a stripper wasn't worth it if she had none of her personal things to show for it. No art work, makeup, clothing...

She needed to get out. Now.

Jude forced her feet to move and ran into a solid object. She pounded her fists. The scent of pine and cigarettes curled around her brain. "Let me out of here!"

Thick fingers encircled her arms. "Jude, honey, it's me."

She knew that voice and that scent. Corey. She inched away from the hulking bouncer. "What are you doing here?" Jude smoothed the wrinkles in her T-shirt and cursed her vulnerable state. Her ire rose. "It's gotta be way past midnight. Why are you outside my door? You live on the top floor next to Tiny."

Corey smothered her in a hug. "I heard your scream, baby. You know I'll come running when you yell."

"She didn't scream."

Jude backed away from Corey. "Ramon?"

Ramon elbowed past the bouncer. "Are you hurt?"

She nodded. "I'm fine, but the apartment's a mess." Tears once again streamed down her cheeks. Why did she always seem to turn into a puddle of mush when Ramon came around? Because, despite the things he didn't say, she cared about him. Yet, all he seemed to care about was who wanted to trash her apartment.

As if he sensed her inner turmoil, Ramon wrapped his arms around her and rubbed her back. He kissed the top of her head. "You're safe now." He spoke over his shoulder. "Call Tiny and tell him what happened."

Corey huffed. "You don't give orders, Decker. That's my job. Besides, we call him Mr Balthazar."

Ramon went rigid around her. Jude leant back within his embrace. "Corey, please? I'll be fine until you get back."

The bouncer snorted and stomped into the hallway.

Ramon folded his arms tight around her once more. "You're coming home with me." He stroked her hair. "I can't risk losing you. Go back to my apartment and wait. I'll make sure there's no one here."

Jude pushed away from him. "No. This is my home. I can take care of myself. Who do you think you are? The police? Tiny will decide how to proceed if he doesn't know already. Really, I'll be fine." She knelt to right her tackle box and replace the scattered and broken conte crayons.

Ramon crouched next to her. He handed her some crushed charcoal pieces and said nothing. A lump formed in her throat. Where was she going to go? Tiny would probably want to check things out. He wielded absolute power and didn't take kindly to people butting in.

Footsteps thumped behind her and Corey rushed back into the room. "Decker, you and I are supposed to clear the apartment. Ross is on his way." He turned to Jude. "Balthazar wants you safe. He wants you to wait in my apartment with Andie. She'll keep you company until I get this cleared up."

She stood and braced her feet a shoulder's width apart. "No." Both men turned in tandem. "I refuse to leave my home."

Corey folded his tattooed arms. "You can't be here."

Ramon dropped his head. "As much as I dislike this clown, I agree. You can't be here."

Tension filled the room. Corey glared at Ramon, while Ramon raked his fingers through his hair. As if to give everyone space, Ross knocked on the open door instead of walking in. "Corey, go to Mr Balthazar's room and let him know I've arrived and then you're free to go home. Mr Balthazar feels the situation is now under control."

Corey nodded his head sharply. "I'm watching you, Jude. This isn't over."

Jude dropped her head into her hands. "I hope it is."

Corey crossed the room and yanked her aside. "I want to help you." His breath heated her ear, making her squirm. "He ain't right, Jude. There's something about him. He's off."

"Ramon's a bouncer at the club, just like you."

"No."

Corey's curt answer shocked her and sent shivers through her body. She brushed him back. "Go home. I'll be fine. I always am."

Corey jerked away from her and glared at Ramon. "Whatever." He gave Ramon the finger and stalked out of the apartment.

Jude raked her fingers through her hair. "He's infantile, but he's loyal." She glanced around the room. "And this is a certified disaster." Her chin quivered and her resolve crumbled. "Who would do this, Ramon? Why?"

Tears rolled down her face, stinging her skin. She caught sight of Ramon's clouded expression. *I can't let him see me cry.* She turned away. "Never mind. Just go away."

"No."

Her voice cracked. "What?"

"I'll fix this."

Jude swallowed and dried her face. "How? You're just a bouncer, not the police. Beyond that, you don't love me, so you have no say in this situation."

Ramon clenched his jaw. She must have hit a nerve and the small victory softened the severity of the moment. She shook her head, looking at the mess. "I'll have to rework my portfolio."

"Jude, you need to give me a chance. Please?" he whispered. "I can fix this."

She fought the urge to buy into his plea. "I'd love to believe you."

"This is a cluster fuck." Ross took up the doorway. His brows knotted as he surveyed the damage. "You're needed upstairs, Decker."

"I'll be right back," Ramon said and shuffled past Ross.

Ross folded his arms and leaned against the doorframe. "Well, what happened?"

"My apartment's been ransacked," she groused. "I'll be here until I'm fifty just cleaning it up. Look around. You can't miss it."

He crouched next to her. "Why don't you find somewhere else to stay?"

"You, too?" She plopped down on her butt. "This is my home. What's it with you men telling me where the hell I can stay?"

"Ramon is unattached and trustworthy. He will protect you."

"Yeah, he's trustworthy and heartless." She tossed a broken chalk stick across the room. "I'll follow him straight to hell."

"Stop." Ross grabbed her arm. "Make amends with him. Yes, he's blunt and he's curt, but he's in your corner."

Ross wasn't one to show emotion and he rarely raised his voice. Jude closed her eyes. "Fine."

"Go." Ross stood and pulled her into a standing position.

Jude stomped down the hall and stood in front of Ramon's apartment. Part of her wanted to slug him. Another part of her wanted to run away. The rest of her wanted to go to sleep and wish the whole damned situation away. She rapped her knuckles on the door.

Ramon strode down the hallway. "Hi, hon. Let me open the door for you. I'm supposed to have you stay with me tonight."

"I don't want to know who decided that for me. I'll sleep on the couch." She stepped into his apartment and stopped. This was too close to being a couple again. "It's only right since we're not together."

"I disagree."

Jude whirled around. "Oh, you do? I won't sleep with a man who doesn't care for me and is acting out of duty to his superior."

"Let me explain..."

Jude gritted her teeth. "No need. I see everything clearly. I'll sleep on the couch until Ross gets my apartment sorted out. Period."

Ramon closed the door and stepped in front of her. He took a deep breath and cupped her chin. Shock rocketed through him that she didn't back away. "I can't protect you when you're out here alone. If you come with me, I can." She looked away. Ramon cocked his head to regain her gaze. Fear and panic registered in her eyes. "Someone wants something from you, Jude. I want them to go through me before they hurt you."

Her chin quivered. "So you can hurt me first?"

"Babe."

Jude jerked out of his grasp and plopped down onto the couch. She tugged the crocheted blanket over her body. "I refuse to sleep with you. You want me only for sex. I put my heart on the line and you smashed it. Not a second time. Go away. I can protect myself."

Ramon threw his hands in the air and stalked into the bedroom. He glanced around the lonely space. Jude's essence permeated the room. Her scent marked his pillows. Her things cluttered the bathroom. Her love—thin at the moment—wrapped around his heart. He rubbed his eyes. Did she love him, or just the character Ramon?

The light in the living room flicked off, bathing the apartment in darkness. Ramon sat on the edge of the bed. Ramon's decree had nothing to do with his feelings. His affection for Jude urged him to protect her. He took a deep breath. Anger or not, he couldn't stand to be apart from her. He strode into the front part of the apartment. What could he say? He needed to rebuild her trust.

He squatted next to the couch. Jude shifted, yet remained silent.

"Deal."

Jude looked at him with questions in her blue eyes. "With what?"

Ramon scooped her into his arms and carried her into the bedroom. Jude thumped his chest, squirming within his grasp. Undeterred, he dumped her on the bed.

"What are you doing?"

"You're right. No sex. But I want us to act as a couple." *I need you too much.* He bit down hard on the tip of his tongue. Admitting his truths wasn't going to win him points with her. Still, it couldn't hurt to try. Putting space between them, he sat on the edge of the bed. "I care about you, very much, Jude. You're a sweet girl, a fantastic lover, and an inspiring artist. I'm a better man when you're with me and I don't want to lose that. I don't want to lose you."

Jude considered him a moment. She knotted her fingers together. Did she want to reach for him? "You got me."

Relief flooded into his mind. "You want to make love?"

Jude rolled her eyes. "You never give up, do you?"

"Never."

She fell back against the pillow. "Then go to sleep with your pyjamas on."

Twenty minutes later, Jude fell asleep with her back to him. The desire to spill his secrets and feelings battled with the knowledge that more hidden cameras lurked in his apartment. Who would overhear the specifics of his job if he revealed his true identity? Tiny and anyone else who wanted dirt.

Ramon stroked her hair. A lump formed in his throat. She deserved the love in his heart. When Jude rolled into his arms and snuggled against his chest, Ramon allowed himself to drift to sleep. If she cuddled, she didn't hate him. If she didn't hate him, there was a chance they could survive the roadblock. If that happened, they could forge a future together. He needed that future. He needed her.

Chapter Seven

Ramon spent the next four days observing and protecting Jude. He remained at a safe distance. Although she stayed with him, her fear and independent streak kept him just beyond reach. At the same time, he immersed himself more fully in the drug trade within the club. Most of the dancers delivered the condom packets. His bar tab reflected the extra purchases. Ramon made notes and reported to Wallace via text messages and personal meetings.

After he dropped Jude off at the college, Ramon met with Wallace and Mateo at the Curry-n-Carry Deli in Crawford, Ohio. He slid into the booth and unzipped his hooded sweatshirt. The thick plastic creaked and groaned with each movement.

Wallace stirred his coffee. The spoon clinked against the ceramic cup. "I see you became close with the dancers. According to Kenworth, you have a favourite."

Mateo snorted. "Close? Favourite? Shit. He's screwing around. I hope your lady friend's a good lay."

Ramon growled. As much as he respected his best friend, sometimes friends needed a swift kick in the ass. "You want to do the job for me?"

Wallace sipped his coffee and his gaze vacillated between the two officers. "I wonder if you know what you're doing."

"I do." *I'm in over my head and in love with a woman I can't have in the end.* "You worry about dickhead here screwing up his traffic detail."

"Me screw up? Nah." Mateo burst out laughing. "But you'd better keep that 'I do' phrase in mind."

"Why?"

Wallace folded his napkin. His moustache bobbed as he wiped the corners of his mouth. "She's under your skin."

Irritation flowed through Ramon's veins. "I can walk away." *I think.* "It's not as complicated as it looks."

"Yeah?" Mateo drummed his fingers along the edge of the Formica. "Why didn't you leave her alone when Malsam cleared her apartment? You let her sleep in your bed like a good, pussy-whipped man. I'm telling you, you're wrapped around her little finger, man."

"I'm concerned." *And in love. Damn it.*

Wallace pinched the bridge of his nose. His salt and pepper brows knotted together and he sighed. "Are you going to be able to nab him? You don't have much time left. He's going to get wise if you piss around."

"I'm working up to him. The girls are the main distributors. Tiny only deals directly to specific clients. I can see it in his eyes he wants to sell to me, but the bastard's being careful."

Mateo slapped his hands on the table. "Then force his ass! Kiss up to another dancer and get her to convince him. You're slipping and we're wasting time. We can't afford to find someone else dead because of his shit cocaine."

"I will." *If I can convince Jude it means nothing...*

"Take my advice, since I don't usually get involved in your personal life." Wallace tapped his finger on the table top. "Forget your piece of ass and get the job done."

Drew shifted back into his Ramon persona and nodded. He slid away from the booth. Because of his job, her heart was shredded. Because of lies he couldn't cop to, her trust in him was shaky. Now he had to toss her aside in order to seal the deal. Shit.

* * * *

Ramon drove across town to the community college campus. He pulled into one of the parking spots lining the street. Jude sat on a bench with her sketch pad open. She'd folded her legs beneath her and her skirt flared around her hips.

"Hi."

She looked up. A small smile flashed upon her lips before fading. "Hello, shadow. Funny seeing you in the daylight."

Ramon shoved his hands into his pockets. "Well, at least you spoke to me. It's a start."

"I know how to be civil." Jude closed the pad and folded her hands. "Do you know where the Ryman Building is?"

He nodded to the building on the hill. "North campus."

She placed the spiral drawing pad in her backpack and stood. "Let's take a walk."

"Lead on."

Jude grinned as she fell into step with him. Her hands swung at her sides. Ramon itched to take her hand in his. Would she inch away? Would she slap him? Would she give in? He rubbed his sweaty fingers against the leg of his jeans and reached for her. Although she didn't look at him, she squeezed his hand...and didn't pull away.

At the doors to the Ryman Building, she stopped. "I want to show you something. Are you game?"

Ramon stood on the bottom step. "I get it. You want to have your wicked way with me on campus." He shook his head. "I'm yours. Find the nearest empty classroom and take me."

Jude raked her free hand through her hair and visibly suppressed a chuckle. "You're incorrigible. You know that, right?"

"It's why you like me."

"I suppose." She shoved the thick glass door open. "Come on."

Ramon cheered his small victory and followed her lead. Jude walked a couple of paces ahead of him. Her ass swayed and turned his insides to jelly. His mouth watered and he flexed his fingers, ready to capture her in an embrace. Just to touch her and feel her silky smooth skin under his. He needed his Jude fix.

She stopped in front of a frosted glass door. "You wanted to see my artwork, correct?"

Ramon came to a halt behind her and twirled a lock of her hair between his fingers. "I seem to recall asking that, yes."

Jude turned the knob. "This is my studio. Not even Tiny knows about it. No cameras, no peepers, nothing."

Ramon eased past her into the room. Although not much bigger than a nine by nine cell, the space sported a wall of windows, bathing the room in natural light. A storage unit with four shelves housed her supply boxes. Next to the door sat a tall filing cabinet with long flat drawers. The scent of paint and fixative hung persistently in the air. He glanced at the photos tacked on to the corkboard and the painting on the nearby easel. Her knack for capturing personality in her subjects was uncanny. "Beautiful."

She took a deep breath and nibbled her bottom lip. "This is my sanctuary. I come here when I need to think and escape."

Ramon opened a portfolio case. The image staring back at him made him pause. She'd captured him at the club on paper. His breath caught in his throat. He looked like Drew—the real man—tired, interested and in awe.

Jude slapped her hands over the image and wrestled to close the black portfolio case. "You weren't supposed to see that one."

He cupped her cheek. A bit of the chalk from the drawing smeared on her creamy skin. He didn't care. To him, she was perfect with smudges. "Was that handsome hunk supposed to be *moi*?"

Crimson streaked across her face, from her hairline to her chin. "Maybe."

"Why wasn't I supposed to see that? What are you trying to hide?"

She stared at her hands. "Nothing."

He dipped his head to meet her gaze. "Your artwork has a little bit of heart in each line. You can't hide that. When I look at that image, I see more than just me. I see the vulnerability of a woman who knows what she wants and can't have it. Few artists can achieve that much emotion in one piece, let alone every creation."

Her smile wobbled. "You really worked hard on that delivery, didn't you?"

Ramon chuckled. "Did it work?"

Jude toyed with the strings on his sweatshirt. "A little."

He pressed a kiss to the corner of her mouth. "Good, because I need all the help I can get. I'm sorry I got so...me on you. I'm trying to protect you the only way I know how."

"I appreciate it, even if I'm a brat." Her shaky breath warmed his skin to fever. He slid his hand down her arm to twine their fingers as she rested her head on his shoulder. "Make love to me where no one can see. No cameras, no voyeurs."

Ramon eased down onto the drawing horse and pulled her onto his lap, facing him. He tucked a loose lock of her hair behind her ear. Every time he thought he had her pegged, she knocked him for a loop. "I'd love to do whatever you want."

"But you won't." Her gaze fell to her hands.

"Sweet girl." He rubbed his forehead against hers, forcing her gaze to his. "This is your special place. I don't want you to do something you'll regret."

Jude worked open the fly on his jeans and caressed his cock. "I've got condoms in my bag. Just bought them."

He shivered and cupped her jaw. "From…?" How the hell was he thinking straight when she was massaging his cock? His eyelids drooped.

"The student centre. Crazy the things they sell there." Jude eased her skirt up, revealing a silky black thong. "I live to surprise you." Her eyes glittered as she tore open the packet then rolled the condom down his shaft. She pulled the tiny lingerie to the side and lowered herself onto his dick. "This is where we belong—in each other's arms."

Truer words were never spoken. He surged up into her slick heat and nuzzled her neck, groaning. "Mine." Instead of thrusting, he remained nestled within her. Nothing mattered except loving her.

"Ramon…"

The sound of his name on her lips brought him down a bit from his high. Ramon threaded his fingers in her hair, pulling her in for a kiss. "I'm going to blow in a second."

"Then do it," she said with a grin.

Ramon slapped her ass and surged into her body. His breathing quickened and a bead of sweat slid between his shoulder blades. Fuck, three thrusts and he'd be done.

She squeezed him with her inner muscles.

"Fuck," he murmured and emptied his seed into the condom.

Jude snuggled into his arms and shivered. "Quick, but worth it."

He stroked her back. Walking away from her would be the hardest thing he'd ever have to do… "I need to get you home to change for work."

Jude sat up straight and brushed her hair from her eyes. "I saw it. Them."

"Who?" Ramon cupped her cheek. *She couldn't be talking about...* "What did you see, babe?"

"Slade and Astra." She stared at her hands. "I don't know who killed them, but I saw her hand and his shoe."

"Where?"

Instead of answering right away, she picked at her ring. Her voice wavered and her body trembled. "I wanted to tell you here where I could trust you and no one would hear."

Ramon crushed her in his grasp. The terror radiating in her being consumed him as well. "Tell me when you're ready. I promise. I won't let anyone hurt you."

"I don't know who did it, but they were in the compactor. No one knows I saw. I emptied the waste cans backstage and they were there." She stared him straight in the eye and tears shimmered on her cheeks. "She was my friend."

Her revelation changed the game. They'd suspected the compactor, but without someone inside he couldn't check. If Tiny or Corey, the baboon, found out she knew... *Fuck.*

"You won't tell. Promise me." Her voice rose three octaves. "Please. I can't quit, but I can't keep that secret anymore. It gives me nightmares."

"Your secret's safe with me, babe." He stroked her hair. No more games with the asshole. Ramon rapidly worked through the scenarios. If he told her his true identity, he risked the wrath of Tiny when he found out. The drug lord wasn't above killing one cop—another cop would be nothing to him. Hurting Jude would just be collateral damage to Tiny. And she mattered too much to him to take the chance. "Let's go home. We'll come up with something to get rid of the darkness." *I have no other choice.*

* * * *

Jude woke the next morning with a start. She gasped for air. The vision of Astra's hand became crystal clear in her head—dull grey and limp. She could almost hear Astra cry. *And...I did nothing.* She sat up and grabbed for the sheets, anything to hide from the darkness. The fear from the break-in slammed into her brain, compounding her anxiety.

She forced her eyes open and stared at her surroundings. Still in the Sanborn in Ramon's room. His gentle rustling beside her reminded her she wasn't in any danger. The visions weren't real any longer. He cared for her and she belonged. "I am safe," she murmured. "I am safe."

"Good morning, sweet girl. You had a nightmare?" Ramon wrapped an arm around her. "You're shaking."

"Good morning, handsome." Jude rolled over to meet his gaze. Her heart melted. His eyes were still heavy with sleep, but completely focused on her and comforting her. "I did, but it's all good now. I've got to get it out of my head that someone's going to hurt me and it's hard, but you're helping so much more than you know." She met his mouth with a wet kiss. He tasted like toothpaste. "What's on the agenda for today? I have an art history class and my last drawing class of the week. Will you be my chauffeur?"

Ramon's laugh wasn't his normal hearty chuckle. Confusion and something else clouded his eyes. "My plan was to screw you senseless and *then* whisk you away to meet some of my family before insisting we marry over in Atlantic City... Unless you have a better idea."

"I see." Jude paused to turn his words over in her mind. He was serious about love and marriage, but when would his emotions change? She shoved the thought aside in favour of vanquishing the darkness. She rubbed her bare breasts on his smooth chest in a move she'd learned from watching Andie on stage. Apparently, the writhing worked for Ramon.

"Come here and let me love you," he said in a thick, sexy voice. "Babe, you're beautiful."

Jude sucked in a ragged breath. Did this man ever tire? She didn't care.

"Come here," he said again.

"Not until I can play with you." She laced her fingers around his morning wood. "You're way ahead of me. No fair." Jude licked her lips and shook her head. With the pad of her index finger, she traced the vein running along the underside of his dick. "Very nice." She bent down and flicked the sensitive tip with her tongue. "You taste sinful."

Ramon shivered and groaned once more. His fingers twined in her hair and he groaned. "Babe, come here before I go off too early. Again."

Ahh, she was on the right track.

Clamping her lips around his heated flesh, she pumped up and down. "Ummm." She took him to the very back of her throat, slowly sucking and teasing around him.

His hips bucked against her skilled assault. "Yeah." His response drove her wild. "No more, babe. I want to be inside you," he rasped.

Very slowly, Jude ran her tongue along the base of his shaft, before sliding up to align their bodies. Once away, she missed his taste. "Okay, you win. But I get to finish later."

He grasped her hips and guided their union. "You will."

Jude reached down and rubbed his dick along her clit. How the man could easily pleasure her body shocked her. "Not yet. I need to catch up to you," she gasped.

Ramon pulled her into his embrace. He licked and sucked on the tender flesh of her neck while teasing her aching nipples. Could sex get better? It seemed so. "Yeah, babe," he groaned.

She looked into his eyes. The deep brown faded into black pools filled with passion only for her. "Ramon." She shivered. "Oh, Ramon!"

Ramon nodded. "I love it when you say my name like that," he said and stroked her silky skin. "Ride me, Jude."

Huh? She'd seen it in the movies, but to actually do it? Wouldn't it hurt?

"I won't hurt you, Jude—you're ready," he said, reading her mind.

Jude lowered herself onto his erect shaft. Her breasts jiggled with each thrust. "Like this?" Good grief—she sounded green. He must think of her as an inexperienced fool.

Ramon's eyes rolled back in his head and he groaned. Jude paused with fear.

"Babe," he rasped. "Oh, yeah. Perfect."

"Oh, God," Jude gasped. The shock of sincere pleasure crashed within her body. Sweet Mother, he was good.

They finished in unison and collapsed together on the bed in a tangled heap.

Ramon ran his fingers through her hair and rubbed her cheek with his thumb. Even her scalp tingled at his touch.

"I meant it, you know."

Jude snuggled up next to him. He spoke, but she really didn't catch the words.

"What?"

"I planned on moving your things down here this morning, meeting some of my close friends and getting married next weekend. Once the boys meet you, I'm sure they'll love you."

Shocked, Jude looked at him blankly. "Get real," she said and tried her best to sound bored. In her chest, her heart pounded triple time. She wanted him to be serious. Was he serious? Married? Saddled down? Forever? And what was the deal with his friends?

"I'm very much for real," he said. "Ray and Logan are great guys. They'll want to get to know the woman in my heart."

Jude's jaw dropped and she felt the blood drain from her face. "Wait... I need to get approval from them? Or are you talking about something else? I don't do free dances and I'm not going to have a ménage to make you look like a badass. Is that what you want?" She wasn't about to be used by another man. Jude sat up and wrapped the sheet around her body. Her hands trembled.

Men could be real pigs, but she'd never expected Ramon to be one. Okay, sure he was a bouncer and a little rough around the edges, but to pass her around? Or was she letting her fear run away with her?

"Slow down, babe." Ramon placed his hand on her arm, stopping her movements. "Can I explain?"

She clutched the bedding but peered at him through loose strands of her hair.

Ramon scooted next to her and smoothed the locks of her hair between his fingers. "I don't mean a ménage or anything else to make me look cool or badass or whatever. I don't know if I could share you with anyone and I know I couldn't handle seeing you with someone else if we split. I only wanted to take you out on a date where my friends hang out. Nothing more." Ramon cupped her chin. "Let's start getting your valuables. I don't want to leave you alone any longer than I have to."

Jude knew they were moving too fast, but her heart and her brain refused to apply the brakes. Her guts screamed this was the right thing to do — move in permanently, offer her love and sacrifice her heart. She scrambled from between his legs and pinned his chest under her knees to slow down. Mussed curls hung around her face. "I have my most treasured valuable right here," she said and jabbed his pecs with her index finger. "But I'd like to move what's left of my security box and art supplies down here, if that's your idea."

Ramon kneaded her ass in his hands. Jude wondered what he might say next.

"That was the plan, love. We can shower once we're done. I love you, Jude."

She'd watched his lips form the words and felt his renewed erection warming her backside. Somewhere between the lust and passion was something else, but what? He had to be joking. He'd said he didn't deal in emotions like love.

"You do?"

Surrender and surprise shone in his eyes. "I care about you and I don't want you working at that shitty club. Please?"

She shrank away from him. Wanted her to quit? Yeah, sure...and money for tuition would just appear? Come on. "Please don't. You're asking things I can't make happen."

"You can do whatever you put your mind to, but I stand behind whatever you want to do." Ramon slipped out from under her and disappeared into the bathroom, leaving her alone.

Jude glanced around the room. As much time as she'd spent in his arms and his bed, she really didn't know him. What made him tick? Why did he want to work at a sleazy nudie bar? With his muscles and commanding tone, he'd make a better cop. She bit down hard on the inside of her cheek and strolled across the room to the window. As she stared out at the city below, she mulled over the past few hours. She'd told him her deepest secret and he'd barely blinked—no, he'd asked her to marry him.

Part of her wanted to go along with his idea. Being a student full-time sounded heavenly. But what if they didn't make it? What if he lost interest and found someone new?

She rested her forehead on the cool glass. One day her world would be less complicated. It had to be. One day.

* * * *

Four trips back and forth in the hallway succeeded in moving all of her things save for the mattress and bulky couch. Jude nudged it unsuccessfully with her hip, making Ramon chuckle.

"Later," he said and pulled Jude into an embrace. "Right now, I need some Jude love. Lock this door and let's get into our shower." He swatted her ass and nearly skipped back to his apartment, caught up in a 'walking on sunshine' moment.

"Where were we?" she asked as he closed the door.

Ramon turned around but before he could answer, she tugged the sweaty T-shirt over her head, releasing her breasts to the cool air. Her nipples instantly sprang to life, insisting on his immediate attention. "Oh, now I remember. You wanted to have sex."

His jaw opened and shut without sound. Hard work turned her on? Who knew? He could definitely get used to this. Her energy would be the death of him and he welcomed the challenge with open arms.

"I'm sorry," she said and strutted over to him. Jude clasped her hands behind her back, inching her breasts forward into his chest. Her head tilted back and her eyes flashed. "Did you have something else you wanted to say?"

Involuntarily, Ramon's hands groped her naked flesh. "I don't remember," he said clumsily and claimed the pale skin of her throat. "Damn, you're a tease—a sex-kitten, but definitely a tease." So he was laying it on a bit thick. Who cared?

Jude groaned and wrapped her arms around his shoulders, digging her nails into his skin. "Oh…"

"Have I told you lately that you're beautiful?" Ramon loved to make her squirm with delight. She knew how to tease him and he loved it. "Damn, you're smokin', woman."

Jude chewed on her kiss-swollen bottom lip and sucked in a ragged breath. "You're not too bad yourself, Mr Decker." She arched into him, rubbing her feverish body against his. "Oh," she sighed. "Yeah."

Ramon raked his fingers along her ribcage. She met him touch for touch on a dizzying emotional high. He loved her and her effect on his whole outlook. "Come on," he coaxed. "I have surprises waiting for you."

She followed him into the hot shower. "Lead on and I'll follow," she said and kissed his chest. "I'd follow you anywhere."

God, please let me be that lucky, he prayed. He'd been too forward, asking her to quit her job, but damn. If she stayed, she'd be in the line of fire. The truth would come out—what she knew and had seen. He could lose her. Ramon pushed the thought aside. He made sure to soap and rinse every inch of her body, adding kisses and squeezes whenever possible. After the shower, he followed her naked form into the bedroom.

"Come away with me tonight." His chest tightened. "We'll go on a date."

Jude unzipped her portfolio case "Ramon, it's Sunday night. Where can we go? I have classes in the morning."

He dropped to one knee beside her and whispered in her ear. "I'm tired of being watched and I want to get away. I thought we'd visit some of my friends and their band. I'll fill you in along the way. Are you game?"

Chapter Eight

Jude twirled in Ramon's arms. Going to the Ricochet had been Ramon's best idea yet. The glittery lights and the stale smoke reminded her of the Silver Steel, but the feeling was totally different. People laughed, drank and cuddled—not a drooling, groping, inebriated man in sight. Being at the Ricochet was like being at a huge barn dance with a couple of hundred friends. She rested her head on his shoulder as Ramon sang along to the band. His throaty rumble made her thighs heat. The last strains of the song reverberated around her chest.

For the first time in a long time, she felt like a normal woman on a normal date with the man of her dreams, not a stripper with a dead-end bum intent on grabbing her assets.

"Here they come." Ramon gave her shoulder a squeeze. "I'd like you to meet a couple of my good friends. If all goes well, we'll be seeing them a lot more."

She tucked in close, suddenly feeling out of place as the two hulking men approached. If they found out what she did for a living, would they want special treatment? A private show? Or would they run away and laugh at the both of them?

The tall man embellished with tattoos and muscles thrust his hand forward. "My name's Ray. You saw me on the leads up there. Tell me your favourite song and, if we know it, we'll play it for you two." When he shook her hand, his hand literally enveloped hers.

She stared up at him. This guy needed to be the bouncer. Just one look and she was ready to comply with his very command.

"He's such a charmer today." The other man stepped forward. "I'm Corbin. You saw me on the drums. I hope we get to see more of you. Drew's a good guy." He nodded once and strolled away.

Jude's blood ran cold. "Drew? That's the second time it's slipped. I thought you said Drew was your first name and Ramon went in the middle?"

Ramon's eyes widened for a split second. "Yeah. Gramma Edna forgets sometimes. Ray's honestly harmless and Corbin's a flirt. They've probably had a couple to gear up to play. Don't worry about them."

"Hey, my man!" Another man strode towards them. Jude pulled away from Ramon. Something felt off.

"You must be Jude. Ramon's told me all about you. I'm Ned." Ned smiled and folded his hands. "I've known Ramon since we were both in diapers. He's good people."

She shifted and fumbled with the hem of her shirt. Something about Ned spoke of authority, but damn...the anxiety wasn't going away. "It's nice to meet you."

"Ramon—Logan and Cass are backstage. I'm sure Cass would love to meet Jude." He winked. "I'm here if you...you know, need something done."

Her throat ran dry. If he needed? Needed what done? "Ramon?"

"I'll explain later, but he's trustworthy. He's a judge." Ramon nuzzled her neck. "I should take you to meet Cass and Logan. You'll probably be fast friends as she begs for information to enhance her books."

Oh fuck. Her lunch reversed its course. An author, a famous actor and a judge. Great. Ramon had to be friends with a judge. Judges weren't likely to befriend a stripper. And celebrities...they didn't need scandal like her. Did Ned know about what she'd seen? Did he think she'd had a hand in it? God, she needed air. "I need to go to the bathroom."

"He'll protect you, just like I will." Ramon stared deep into her eyes. "Promise. I keep my promises. No one knows."

Jude rested her head on his shoulder and closed her eyes. "I can handle that."

"Excuse me?"

Jarred by the odd tone of his voice, she opened her eyes and kissed his chin. "What did you say?"

Ramon cocked his head. "I didn't say anything."

Another hand touched her arm. "I did."

Before she could respond, Corey stood before her. Miranda clung to his shoulder. "We came to see Hillbilly Boots. Goldie likes their cover of *Change Me*."

Miranda released her grip on Corey and sidled up against Ramon. "You need to share your love."

"I'm good." Ramon cuddled Jude closer. "Did you want something?"

Corey nodded. "I wanted a dance with Judy. Miranda's asked non-stop for one slow song to dance with you, Ramon. It's only fair if we trade."

Jude shared a glance with Ramon. His brown eyes blazed. He didn't seem pleased by the trade idea. She shrugged. "I suppose one dance won't hurt." She held up her index finger. "Just one."

Miranda shoved Jude aside and manoeuvred Ramon across the dance floor, out of view. Jude swallowed past the lump in her throat. A hint of jealousy clouded her vision and the thick musk of Corey's cologne choked her. Maybe the dance wasn't such a great idea.

"You know he's a cop, right?"

Jude balled her fists on his shoulders. "He's not." Even if Ramon was, she didn't care. She wanted far away from Corey but, damn it, she had to play up to him before she'd get an excuse to leave.

"You're blind. He's too rigid and protecting."

She groaned. "Tiny wouldn't hire a cop." But a cop would know a judge. Damn.

Corey cocked a brow. "Tiny's playing with *Ramon*. He knows the truth and wants to see how long it'll be before he fucks up. I doubt his name is even Ramon."

Her heart squeezed within her chest. Corey couldn't be spouting the truth. Could he? Why would Tiny bring in a cop when he was the one crossing the line into illegal activities? She shook her head to dislodge the doubt forming. "He's Ramon Decker. I know. I met his family. Now leave him alone." Little things Ramon had said — the slips of his name, his knowledge of things he shouldn't know about... It made sense for him to be an officer of the law.

"You're so naïve."

She backed away from him. Her mouth went dry. Her tongue tasted bitter and ten sizes too large for her mouth. "Why? Because I won't sleep with you? Because I'm not just blindly following what you said? That's not naïve. God, I lost my friend — your ex-girlfriend—and I'm afraid I'll be next. I'm trying to be cautious."

"Cautious, my ass." Corey folded his arms. "I know you slept with *him*. It's written all over your face and the tapes... Yeah, I see the tapes. You love him and it's unreciprocated. I'll tell you right now that he's not interested in you for anything more than sex. Care to prove me wrong?"

"It's complicated." Jude set her jaw. "Why did you watch? Are you jealous?"

"Complicated, my ass. You know damn well my job is surveillance." Corey grabbed her arms and his fingers bit into her flesh. The muscles ached under the pressure of his touch. "Why won't you believe me?"

"Because you're hurting me." She held as still as possible, hoping he'd release his grip. "What do you want from me?"

"Unload his worthless ass and go to Tiny. Astra fucked up and joined the wrong side. Don't be like her. Let Ramon have the woman he wants." He nodded across the dance floor to where Miranda danced with Ramon. She held him in a tight embrace. His eyes were closed. Did he like her kisses? Did he want Miranda?

"I don't buy it." Jude's stomach churned. She pushed her concerns down deep. First chance she got to run, she'd bolt. "Just let me go."

Corey yanked hard on her chin, refocusing her attention. "Why should I let you go? Because he's sweet to you? Because he's a gentleman? He's an asshole. When you're in *class*, he's fucking around with Miranda. I'd never do that to you. I care about you." He patted her cheek, but the action felt more like a series of slaps. "Why can't you listen to me?"

"Because you're still hurting me!"

"Let her go." The bass voice came from behind Corey. When she looked up, her mouth slid open a fraction of an inch. Ray, the man who embodied strength and muscle, clenched his jaw.

She gasped. "Oh!"

Corey smirked. "It's about time you realised how important I am."

"Important enough to get the fuck out!" Ray slapped his hands down on Corey's shoulders, making the younger man jump. "I don't want your kind of trouble here."

Corey waved his fingers, dismissing the larger man. "Piss off, dude. Get your own lady."

Ray fisted Corey's shirt. He turned and sheltered Jude from Corey's wrath. "The lady said you hurt her. Get out of this dance hall before I have to call the law."

"Let...let me get my date."

Ray shoved Corey in the direction of the door. "She's outside."

Corey tripped, his arms flying forward and his composure slipping. When he stood erect, his lips curled in a sneer. "Alone? Never leave a woman defenceless."

"She'll manage."

"Jackass."

"You'd know." Ray nodded to Jude and elbowed Corey to the exit.

Jude toyed with the strings on her blouse, unsure where to go. She didn't see Ramon or any of his friends. Apprehension and anxiety curled into a tight ball in the pit of her stomach. Being in the middle of the crowd scared her more than Corey's assault.

"Need me?"

She knew that voice. Jude turned and stared at her saviour. *Ned*. "Thank God. Where's Ramon?"

A crooked smile curled the corner of his mouth and a shock of dark hair slipped over his brow. "Over there, looking for you. I'll help you get over to him." He touched her arm. "Trust him."

She paused and placed her hand on his chest. "Why? What's going on that I should know? I don't like being the last to find out what's going to impact me."

Ned pinched his fingers and streaked them across his lips like he was closing a zipper.

"Whatever you say." She patted his forearm. "Just another person who seems to know what's best for me without bothering to tell me what the hell's going on. Fine. I'll find him on my own." With that, she crossed through the throng of people to where Ramon and Ray stood. "Let's go home."

"Jude?" Ramon threaded his fingers with hers.

"What, babe?"

Ned came to a halt beside her. "Damage control."

The colour drained from Ramon's face. So he knew something he wasn't telling? Great. Jude released his hand and stared at the floor. Damn. She wasn't even sure how to get home. No way in hell she'd ask Corey.

"Why don't we head home? Looks like I've got some…kissing up to do." Ramon brushed his knuckles down her cheek. "Please?"

"As long as we're not here, I'll be fine."

* * * *

Ramon gritted his teeth. From the moment they'd left the club and headed to the farmhouse, she'd kept quiet. He yearned to grill her, to find out what the hell they'd let slip. Sure, he trusted Ned, Ray and Corbin.

The guys were like his brothers. But then Corey had had to show up. And fucking Miranda. They knew something, but what had they told Jude?

Instead of coming right out and asking her, Ramon stared at the blank television screen. He had to say something.

Jude strolled into the bedroom, hair damp from her shower. Her skin glowed with tiny droplets of water on her shoulders. "Do you always watch television without it turned on?" She tugged the towel from her hair and plopped down onto the edge of the bed. "They make these things called remotes. They turn the thing on and even change the channels without you having to move an inch. You should try it."

"What would I do without you, smarty pants?"

"End up with a statuesque blonde, living in the 'burbs and making lots of kids. You'd slave at the club at night while she spends your money on diapers, formula and sex toys."

He followed her logic right up to the sex toys. "Really? And why would we need the toys?"

"Low stamina."

Ramon jerked up from his seat and crossed around the bed. It wasn't the comment per se that irritated him. She gave him fits regularly. He knew his performance in bed wasn't an issue either. What pissed the hell out of him was her flippancy. She didn't want to talk about the chasm between them any more than he did. Well, tough shit. He took both her hands in his. She crooked one brow but didn't say anything.

"I should spank your ass for being difficult."

"I'd like it."

"I know." He pinned her hips between his thighs. "Which is why I won't, but I want to talk to you. What did Corey say?"

She closed her eyes. "He mentioned you might be a cop."

"Do you believe him?"

"I don't know." She opened her eyes. "I... Some of it makes sense. You seem to know everything and everyone. You can't stand it if you're not in control. If you're not watching me, you're not happy."

"And that makes me a cop?"

"No. Nosy maybe...observant and cautious."

"There's something else going on here. Tell me."

"I feel safe with you, like I can tell you anything, but I'm scared it's coming back to bite me in the ass. Corey... He's Tiny's right-hand man. If he thinks something is hinky, he'll..."

"Turn us in?" Ramon slid off the bed and stood before her. Corey would have to be the chink in the armour. Fine. "He can't touch you. I won't let him."

She nodded and stared off to the side as she snatched her sleep shirt from the end of the bed. "I just wanted a normal life. I don't want to keep taking my clothes off for men, skirting illegal shit and putting myself in danger." She yanked the cotton shirt over her head and stuck her arms through the sleeves. When she stood, she removed the towel. "I want a stable life with a guy who cares about me in a little house where I'm safe and cherished."

Ramon took the towel from her hands and tossed it onto the armchair. "Let's rest. It's been a long night."

Shoulders slumped, Jude climbed into bed. She kept her back to him and snuggled under the sheets.

He tore his shirt up over his head and shucked his jeans. The look on her face before she turned away from him ripped his heart into shreds. He eased down beside her. "Come here, please?"

She didn't jump when he asked. Instead, she made him wait. Jude's eyes shimmered in the low light.

"What if I could make some of your dreams come true?"

"How?"

He wrapped her in his arms. "If you could decorate the farmhouse any way you wanted, how would you?"

"This isn't your house."

"Gramma lives with me, but she signed it over to me about five years ago. So, decorate for me. What would our room look like?"

Jude curled against him, nice and tight. She twined her leg with his. "Blue walls."

"Yeah? Navy or pale?"

"Dark with white trim. I'd put a mirror over the headboard and make sure the furniture matched."

"You don't like my early bachelor look?"

She giggled and her breath fanned over his chest. "I've always wanted a sleigh bed, lace curtains and a view of the sunset."

He buried his nose in her hair, breathing deeply of her essence. A sleigh bed had definite possibilities. Lace wasn't his style, but making her happy seemed to suit him at every turn. "Would you live here with me?"

"I'd go anywhere with you," she murmured. Her body sagged against his as she drifted to sleep. Her hand fell slack on his chest.

Ramon closed his eyes. She might not be awake to hear his grand confession, but he couldn't hold back any longer. "My name is Drew. I'm a cop, I'm in love with you...and I'm about to lose you."

Instead of the weight lifting from his shoulders, it settled down heavier than before. Tears burned behind his eyelids. He wasn't sure who would hear his prayer, so long as someone cared. *Just don't let me fuck it up when she walks.*

Chapter Nine

Ramon stared at the streak of sunlight arched across the ceiling. In the twenty years he'd lived in the farmhouse, he could've sworn he'd never seen the light arc in such a fashion. Looking at it almost made him want to draw again. Being with Jude nudged him towards going back to his hobby. When was the last time he'd put pencil to paper?

He grinned. The last time he'd indulged in drawing had been the quick sketch he'd made of her at the police station during the initial briefing. Had it been a sign? Perhaps.

Jude sighed next to him and pressed her ass into his hip. The action both infuriated and intoxicated him. Too many nights of sleeping alone made him long for the fullness of the bed, while the gentle nudging reminded him of all he cared about when he held her in his arms. A feeling he could easily lose if she found out his truths. A crazy thought popped into his head. They had all afternoon and all the privacy in the world at the farmhouse. If he wanted more than a fleeting memory…

"You're thinking really hard." Jude giggled, her back to him. "About what?"

"How can you tell?"

She flopped over onto his stomach, pressing her chin into his sternum. "Green smoke filling the room. When you think, green smoke comes out your ears."

He hitched her sleep shirt up over her hips and palmed her ass. "Tell me what I'm thinking about, if you're so slick."

"I am slick." She wriggled, capturing his erection between her damp thighs. "From the tent pole, I'd say you're thinking about sex."

"Possibly later, but not yet. I have a question. You pose for your classes, right?"

She folded her hands under her chin. "You saw me, so that's a yes."

Duh. He laughed to cover his embarrassment. He'd walked in on her being pawed by the frat boy and the moment still rubbed him raw. He shook off the useless frustration. "Will you pose for me? I'll let you work on your project when we're done."

Jude rose up to a sitting position and whipped her sleep shirt up over her head. "I'd love to. I know you'll respect me when it's over."

He'd always respect her. "Wear my dress shirt."

Her eyes flickered with mischief and interest. "I didn't think you wore formal clothes."

He nodded to the closet. "Grab one of the pinstripe ones and leave it unbuttoned. I want a hint of mystery mixed with innocence and sexuality."

She glanced over her shoulder. "You don't demand much, do you?" Jude removed a shirt from the hanger and draped it across her shoulders. Her eyes closed as she ran her fingers down the line of buttons. "So soft."

Ramon stood and crossed the room. Seeing her in the dark fabric, wrapped up in the real Drew, pushed his emotions farther into uncharted territory. He'd loved before, but never as much as he cared for her.

"Here." Ramon arranged her beside the French door. "Okay?"

Jude nodded. Ramon grabbed the sketchbook and a pencil. He visually caressed her body, memorising every curve and plane. Each line, each mark, brought him closer to her and closer to admitting the truth. Once the operation ended, he'd have to make a choice—if he followed his heart, he'd have her forever. If he followed the rules of the job, he'd be alone for the rest of his life. The corners of his eyes burned as he finished the sketch. Letting her go would certainly be the death of him. He forced a smile to his face. "Come here." He smoothed his hand over the page. "Do you like?"

Jude plopped down next to him. She clasped her hands in front of her mouth as if she needed to pray or hide her own smile. "I love it. You should get a degree. You have serious talent."

He shrugged. "No patience. I'd rather doodle."

She dropped onto the bed next to him and rested her head on his shoulder. "If that's a doodle, I'd be willing to bet a concentrated effort would knock my socks off."

"You aren't wearing socks."

She thumped his arms. "You knew what I meant. You'd be fantastic."

"I'll leave fantastic to you." He tossed the drawing pad on the nightstand. "Let me hold you."

Jude stood. She wriggled out of the shirt, letting it slide down her arms.

"Stop."

She froze. "Why?"

"You look too good in my shirt to strip you naked. Downright sexy."

Jude wrapped the shirt around her body and climbed into bed next to him. "I have a question for you."

"Oh, yeah?"

"Are you a cop?"

He clenched his teeth. "What?"

She rubbed her cheek against his collarbone. "Corey warned me while you danced with Miranda. He claims Tiny's one step ahead of you."

Ramon listened as she recalled the conversation. A dull ache grew behind his eyes. Damn it. Corey had to be a little deeper into the system than he'd assumed and evidently wasn't as stupid as he acted. Probably not as high on coke as they'd assumed, too. *Shit, shit, shit.*

"I just want the truth, Ramon."

He drew a deep breath, slow and low so she wouldn't notice. "I'm a complicated man. I want what I can't have and I've made mistakes in my life that I can't correct."

She swirled her fingers in his sprinkling of chest hair. "Like what? It can't be worse than taking your clothes off for strangers. That's mine."

He chuckled. "That is your action to live down…or up to, depending on how you look at it. I think you're doing fine."

"So what do you want?"

"You. I want you, but, when you graduate, you'll see I'm not worthy of you. You'll move on. I can't keep a free spirit chained because I can't let go."

She crawled onto his chest and kissed him hard. "I wasn't kidding."

He sipped her, tasting the evidence of their lovemaking on her tongue. "About what, sweet girl?"

"I love you. Even if you don't love me, I feel that way about you. I don't regret a second of our time together."

* * * *

"Can you grab the sepia contes for me?" Jude sat hunched over her drawing board, working furiously to finish her drawing. "I want to capture this light before we have to head to the club. It's brilliant."

Ramon looked in her tackle box packed full of art supplies. He preferred the simplicity of pencil and pen, but in her hand any art tool looked sexy. He grabbed the first container that said 'sepia' and 'conte'. They all looked the same to him, so he handed her the ruddy brown crayons. "Are these correct?"

"Yep."

"You push me around now, but, babe, I'm going to get mine when you're done." Ramon hadn't really wanted to come back from the farm, but if they'd spent too much time away from the apartment building, no doubt, Tiny would have noticed and probably sent his rat Corey to call.

"Paybacks?" She snickered. "Like…?"

"You'll see, but I'd bet you can guess."

Ramon dug his hands into his pockets and glanced around to soak in the view from the balcony. Carrington Falls wasn't a teaming urban metropolis like other large cities. He could only wonder about what she found so brilliant. To him, the landscape was bleak and industrial. Then again, the last two weeks had made him see lots of things in a different light. Like wanting to indulge in his hobby more often…well, his favourite one other than making love to Jude.

"Look at the way the sunlight bounces off that building." Jude pointed to the old Carlson apartment complex. "The orangey glow is beautiful."

Ramon directed his gaze to the structure in question and then at her drawing. She'd caught the building and the play of light perfectly. "That's amazing."

"I know," Jude replied with a sigh and brushed away a loose strand of hair. "Being on this side of the building, I bet all your sunsets are fantastic. I got to look at a brick wall."

"I meant your drawing." Ramon rubbed her shoulders. He smiled. While he thought about kissing her senseless, she worried about sunsets. For Jude, he'd happily learn to pay attention to simple things like the colours of the leaves and the way her skin broke out in gooseflesh under his caress.

Ramon couldn't keep his hands off her, not that Jude minded. "I've never spent a sunset out here. I wouldn't know what they looked like. When we roll in, it's usually pitch black out."

Jude blew the dust away from her paper, hummed a few bars of a recent country hit, and added a few more details. "Yeah, I guess you're right. Still, it's pretty."

He marvelled at her intensity and focus. Jude worked full-throttle on her drawings like he did on an investigation. Her inner beauty shone as she created. Jude's skin flushed and her eyes became bright. The way she curled around the drawing board stirred his libido and made him love her all the more.

"Have you considered doing portraits for a living? I'd bet you'd be great at capturing inner essence." He rested his chin on her shoulder. "That drawing of me was fantastic. I think the smears add to the drama and show I've changed."

"You can be real deep when you want to." Jude furrowed her brows and turned to look at him. "I drew that a couple of months ago for a design class. We needed 'the perfect model', so I chose you. At the time, you were an enigma to me — so I could transpose whatever I wanted on to your…visage." She wrinkled her nose, then brushed loose hairs away from her face and inadvertently smeared brown conte dust across her cheek. "Do you think this is 'A' material?"

Ramon nibbled her neck. "You caught the light perfectly," he said and indulged on her naked flesh. 'I'd give everything you do an 'A', but, then again, I'm biased."

Jude arched her body, improving his access. "That doesn't help much, but it makes me feel good." She sighed and curled into his touch. "Real good."

"I never lie," he said between searing kisses. "I'll always tell you the truth." *When I can.*

Jude sighed contentedly. "I have to put this away before I ruin it."

Ramon reluctantly released her shoulder. He could chill out for homework.

She placed the drawing in her portfolio case and went back out to pick up her supplies. When she re-emerged from the balcony, Ramon closed the sliding door.

With the arch of one brow and a half-smile, Jude garnered his full attention. She put her hands on her hips, unintentionally arching her chest towards him. "What?"

The simple question goaded him into action. He smoothed Jude's tank top over her head, allowing her breasts freedom. He knelt down in front of her partially nude body. Her nipples puckered in the cool air and his hot breath. She shivered as he tickled the tips with his tongue.

With a fresh conte crayon, he drew a heart over her left breast. Within the heart, he wrote his name. On her stomach, he drew a stick figure. It was supposed to be a baby, but he wasn't the high-calibre artist she was.

Jude giggled. "What are you doing?"

"Claiming what's mine and showing you my art." Ramon grinned, pleased with his artistic rendering. He'd never known art products could be so kinky. Then again, it was probably that Jude was all the kink he needed. Jude sucked in a ragged breath and reached out for his body. Ramon loved that he could make her body react with genuine words of affection.

Jude slid the boxer shorts she'd commandeered from his top dresser drawer down to the floor. "What else do you want to create?"

Ramon licked his lips. "So much perfect skin and so many ideas." He drew a sinewy line on the soft flesh of her inner thigh. "So little time to explore." Instead of continuing the line to her other leg, he planted his face in her pussy. Jude puffed out a slow breath, letting him know she approved.

"Babe, you taste so sweet and hot," he gasped.

Jude shifted her hips. "Your tongue should be insured," she groaned and ran her fingers through his hair.

Ramon sucked at her clit, rolling his tongue along her sensitive folds. His hands smeared the chalky conte on her skin, heightening her arousal. Damn, he could come just listening to her.

"Ramon," she gasped and reached out for stability. His assault on her clit increased. The moan came from deep in her throat. "Oohh."

He continued to flick her sensitive core. She tasted like wine. "Yes, babe—come for me. Come all over me."

"Yes," Jude hissed. Her nails dug into his shoulders. Her head lolled back as the orgasm swept over her body. "Oh, yeah."

A sweet sigh escaped her lips and spurred him on. He needed to hold her, so he guided her to the floor to rest. Could love get any better than this? He brushed her hair away from her face. "Satisfied?"

The ability to speak escaped her. Jude nodded and buried her face in his neck.

"I'll take that as a yes." He cradled her limp body against his.

Love and sex got better and better every time. Jude rocked him to the core and stabilised his life. He could be her safe harbour and soft place to land. And now they had the rest of their lives to revel in each other.

A knock on the door interrupted any further exploration. They exchanged confused looks. Jude slid off his lap to retreat to the bedroom. Ramon wiped the chalk off his hands onto his jeans and stood to go answer the door.

"Just a minute." Ramon wondered who could be on the other side. His stomach roiled with apprehension. By some evil stroke, it could easily be Carlie. Please God, not Carlie. He peeked through the peephole. Nothing. "I could swear someone..."

Ice flowed through his veins. Someone had been out there. Someone wanting to send a message. He clicked the deadbolt and the chain into place. *Fuck, fuck, fuck.*

"What's wrong?" Jude called from the bedroom. "You're talking to yourself again."

"It's nothing. Are you about ready?"

Jude locked the door. "I will be. Hold your horses."

"I will torture you for this." Ramon knocked on the bathroom door. "Long hours of torture with whatever I can find."

"Yeah, right. I'm almost ready."

"About time. You don't have to doll yourself up a lot. I'd prefer naked," he called and unbuttoned his shirt. In his mind, he pictured a myriad slinky negligees adorning Jude's body. Blood rushed straight to his groin. "How about nothing but my hands covering your body? Or my dress shirt?"

"And ruin the surprise? One more minute."

Ramon pressed his ear against the barrier. He could hear her humming an old Beatles song. Something about pleasing him… A smile curled his lips — he'd please her all night and all day too.

"Okay."

The door clicked. Ramon ran his fingers through his hair to compose himself. He felt twice as nervous as he had back at the club. Jude muddled his brains with too much pleasure. He pushed open the barrier.

The soft glow of candlelight illuminated the room. Jude lay sprawled out on the bed, dressed in a red teddy with black lace covering her breasts. Dark curls cascaded down her shoulders and a single strand of pearls dipped into her cleavage. Black thigh-highs and stilettos complemented the look. "Come here." She sat up. "I want to undress you."

Ramon silently complied and stood before her. Jude could do whatever her heart desired.

Jude rose up on her knees. She smoothed the dress shirt away from his shoulders, letting it pool at his feet. Starting on his left nipple and working her way across, she sipped, feasted on his body. Jude hummed before tickling his pectoral muscles with her hot wet tongue. Heat and passion blazed through his veins. Ramon ran his fingers through her hair, massaging her scalp and basking in her skilled assault. Jude leant back out of his grasp and tossed her hair over her shoulders. The gesture drove him wild.

Jude smoothed her hands down his arms. He hardly noticed when she reached around his waist and handcuffed his wrists together. He was too busy feeling and experiencing to notice or care.

She unzipped his trousers, letting them join the shirt on the floor. Dropping to her knees, she brushed her lips on his engorged cock. He shuddered, totally in heaven. He wanted her in his world forever.

As Ramon attempted to grasp for her once more, he realised his immobility. His nostrils flared and his sex soared. "Babe?"

She wanted to be in charge? Hell, yeah. He could share control with Jude. Ramon didn't care as long as they both came away sated. Jude playfully tugged on the waistband of his boxers and he obediently followed her to the edge of their bed.

"I want to dance for you," Jude purred.

If Ramon wasn't hard before, her words sent him into another galaxy. "Yes," he gasped as she stood up.

Jude turned around and tilted her head back. Her hands roamed her body, grazing over her breasts and between her thighs. Everything was done just out of his line of vision. Sweet torment. This was just like his wildest fantasy. No—it was better.

"Babe, turn so I can see you," he pleaded. "I want to join you."

He'd go off like a cannon if she didn't. The steel between his legs shouldn't have been able to get any harder, but somehow it did. She made it hurt so good.

Jude peeked over her shoulder and slipped one thin, red silk strap down. Jude licked then pursed her lips. "Do this?" She turned so he could watch her remove the lace from her breasts. Jude ran the strand of pearls across her tongue, mimicking her intended assault on his cock. "Or this?" Her eyes flashed with smouldering sexuality.

Dear God, he wanted to feel her lips against his skin. He needed her more than air. "Oh, babe." His mouth watered. "Do everything, Jude." Ramon gulped air in ragged breaths. Emotion clouded his mind, making it hard to think straight.

Sensing his impatience, Jude stepped forward enough to prop one foot up on the bed. At that angle, he could easily see that there was no crotch to her teddy. "Do you like what you see?"

Ramon came forward to rub his face against her breasts. Jude smelled like heaven—sweet, soft heaven. She knew she had him teetering on the ragged edge, so she backed away slightly. "Do you want to taste what you see?"

From somewhere deep in his throat, came the guttural reply. "Yes, I'm dying for a taste of you..."

Jude nodded and kissed the tip of her finger before sinking it deep into her folds. Instead of touching his lips with her satiny offering, she licked it off her fingers. He strained against the cuffs. Fantasies didn't get hotter than this. Ramon's body vibrated with need for her.

He nearly came just watching her. "You are one *sexy* tease. Jude, I love you."

Leisurely she unbuttoned the front of the teddy. "Me? You love me?" Jude's sugary sweet smile became instantly fiery and her lips parted. "Because I love you too. I've wanted to hear those words from you since the moment I met you."

He could hear that for the rest of his life. His voice was thick and hoarse. Ramon couldn't hold back, especially when he couldn't hold Jude. "Babe, I can't wait any longer."

She nodded and pushed him back onto the bed. His boxer shorts barely concealed his heat. Gleeful greed filled Jude's eyes. What would she do next? As long as it concerned him, Ramon didn't care. His self-control was officially gone. All he wanted was her.

"Cuffs?"

Jude scampered to the head of the bed. "I'll take care of it...eventually," she whispered in his ear. Ramon's shaft stood rigid, waiting for her attention.

Jude straddled his face and lowered her labia to his lips. Ramon lapped at her clit, intermittently switching between teasing and tormenting her core. His tongue mimicked sex, plunging deep into her canal.

Jude moaned and fumbled with the cuffs. "More work like that and I won't be able to set you free," she gasped and slid the silk boxers past his hips.

Jude's soft lips seared Ramon to the core. She tasted sweet and tangy, like a woman should.

Ramon worked the catch on the cuffs and shifted to pluck her nipples with his newly freed hand. He slapped her bottom with his other hand, making a loud crack. "Yeah," Jude moaned and ground her slit against his lips. "God, yeah."

Her mouth plunged down onto his shaft, matching his rhythm between her legs with her own. Ramon felt her shudder as the orgasm ripped through her body.

She crushed their bodies together for a deeper connection. "Oh, yeah." Her pleasure spurred his need and he slapped her rump once more. Ride the ragged edge. "Come for me, babe. Let it go."

His climax peaked shortly after hers and she greedily suckled his salty offering. Bliss, pure bliss. Jude's body became putty in his hands.

Ramon slid down to stroke her face. "I'm glad you never did that at the club. I don't want to think of any other man seeing you like I did."

Jude kissed his inner thigh, running her tongue along the soft hairless patch. Ramon arched against her, trailing his fingers against her spine.

"For your eyes and hands only," she murmured and met his mouth with a kiss.

He shifted to sit up and coaxed her onto his lap. Her teddy fell away from her body, leaving only the stockings and heels. Ramon's mouth watered and he visually fondled every inch of her being. "Damn, that's a beautiful look for you," he said in a husky voice.

"I prefer you naked," she said parroting his early suggestion.

Ramon licked along her sternum, intentionally ignoring her breasts.

Jude writhed in order to redirect his attention. "Touch me where I need you."

He tickled her tight nipples by blowing warm breath across them. "I want to take my time."

She screamed his name.

Take his time? Not at this rate. Ramon already had another erection.

Jude clasped his head to her breast. "Please."

Ramon suckled deep. He was there and she was close. "Ready to go again?"

Jude nodded then groaned as he slipped two fingers into her sheath. "Yeah."

He grasped her hips and guided her onto his engorged shaft. She jumped slightly as he filled her, becoming one. Her breasts rubbed against his bare chest and her fingers worked through his hair.

"I've never wanted anyone as much as I want you right now," she whimpered. "Take me hard, Ramon. Now."

With little effort, he flipped her over on the edge of the bed and plunged into her hot, slippery canal.

"Babe, I want you too."

Ramon slapped the tender flesh of her rump for a third time. He should've worried about unintentionally hurting her, rather than simply reaching orgasm, but Jude's groans let him know how he turned her on.

Jude's breathing hitched. "Ohh...God," she squealed.

He reached around to capture her breasts in his hands, rolling and pinching her nipples between his deft fingers. Her muscles tightened around his cock as the second orgasm reached its full force. His breath became ragged. Fuck it. He had to tell her how he felt. "I love you, Jude."

Her eyes widened. "You really do love me? Wow."

"I do, babe. I love you."

After a moment, she regained her focus and she gripped him tighter. "I love you, Ramon." Jude arched her back and pressed into him, sending him deeper into her body. Her hips bucked against him. "Fill me, Ramon. I want to feel you in my soul."

Ramon groaned and did as she asked. He collapsed against her back and kissed her neck. Jude sighed contentedly. "This is the best night of my life," she gasped.

He shifted to her side and brushed her tangled hair from her face. He knew that he'd never been truly in love before Jude. Jude was the woman made just for him. "I mean it, love. You're mine."

Tears streamed down her cheeks.

Ramon held her tight against his chest. Tension thicker than pea soup flooded the room. Things didn't make sense. Did she cry because she was happy or shocked? It couldn't be regret, could it?

"What's the matter, babe?" he whispered.

"I don't deserve this," Jude gasped between sobs and shook her head. "I'm not worthy of you."

Ramon wiped her tears away with the pad of his thumb. "Babe, talk to me. Tell me why."

As much as Jude wanted to be happy—she couldn't. When would Ramon laugh? When would he tell her to grow up or walk away in disgust? Men expected things of her—when would he fall into that inevitable trap? Sure, he'd said he loved her…but men changed their minds. He could, too. But, if she didn't come right out and give him the truth, she had no idea what he'd do.

"No one else wanted me." She stared at the floor. "Why *did* you, Ramon? I'm no one. I'm not perfect, not skinny, not…"

He cradled her face in his palms, cutting off her rant. Jude had no idea what he thought and feared his ridicule. His jaw tightened. "Who? Who didn't want you? I'll make it right. Please tell me."

She took a deep breath to calm down. Jude regained her composure and came to a realisation. He wasn't like the men in her past. He was her future. A safe, honest and equal future. "I'm just scared you'll walk. I'm not good at keeping...a man's attention."

"Then he's an idiot."

"Thanks." She snorted to hide the chuckle.

"My pleasure," he soothed. "Take a deep breath and tell me what's on your mind."

Could he handle this? Would he run? Jude didn't want pity, so she decided to lay it all out for him, but hesitated long enough to rake her fingers through her hair. She closed her eyes to prevent more tears. The truth would set them free. It had to.

"You are the first person who's truly wanted me." Jude wiped her face with both hands. Her makeup smeared as the tears flowed. She had earned her freedom from the past and no one could take that away, but maybe Ramon could ease the hurt to a bearable level.

"When I was little, my folks split. Fighting, arguing, split lips, bruises...that sort of thing. When Mom took off to meet the other men, Dad beat the living hell out of me. He thought I looked too much like her. I spent most of my elementary school career with bruises and long sleeves." She paused to catch her breath.

Ramon quietly stroked her cheek. Jude couldn't gauge his expression. She had no idea what he thought and there was so much information to digest. Better press on.

"In court, they asked me who I wanted to go with, Mom or Dad. I was like seven years old. How did I know they were using me? It came down to money — who got child support and who had to shell it out. I didn't know that so I told them that I wanted to live with the both of them and not split. After four years of going from house to house, both parents gave up custody of me. Money was more important."

He gathered her body in his arms. She knew his sigh was out of sheer frustration. He didn't act like he planned to escape. No, he acted like he understood and wanted to take the hurt away. He could be her rock in life.

"I ended up living in the children's home until I was sixteen. For whatever reason, that's when my mother decided that I needed to live with her." Shame settled heavy in her mind. "I never got to date, attend the prom, or do what normal kids my age did. Instead, I found ways to run away and places to hide."

"Why?"

Jude began to rock back and forth in his arms. No one knew her complete story and here she was spilling it with little care. "I ran away at seventeen because she abused me. Nothing physical—her tactic was purely emotional. When I didn't make decent grades, she called me lazy and stupid. Even if I did, the names continued. When I stayed over at school to work on my art projects, she told people I was sleeping with the faculty. If I joined a club, I supposedly did the jocks." Her bottom lip trembled. "My own mother ruined my self-esteem, so I held tight to the only thing I could control. I stayed a virgin to prove I could. Stupid, huh?"

His voice was soft and soothing. "Is that why you began dancing?"

"Not really." Jude nodded and took another deep breath. "I didn't have to think. No one cut me down and I made enough money to be my own person, instead of counting on others for anything. It was all rote. Well, it was until you showed up. I guess I'm more naïve than I thought."

Ramon rocked her gently in his arms and touched his forehead to hers, breathing her in. They would muddle through life together, he'd guarantee it. "You're not naïve or foolish or any of those things you think, but you are safe with me. I promise."

Jude's head dropped against his shoulder in relief. "Looks like we're both damaged goods, huh?"

"It doesn't matter. You're perfect enough for me," Ramon soothed and held her tight.

Jude raised her head to look him in the eye. Ramon barely moved—in fact, he stayed put and smiled. Shock and renewed desire heated her body. "No running away? I haven't scared you into retreat yet?"

"I'm a lot tougher than you give me credit for being." He nuzzled her cheek. "Just give me time to prove it."

Chapter Ten

"We have an hour before we have to leave to get to the club on time." Jude grabbed his hand. "Why don't we go for a walk?"

"A walk? Now?" Ramon furrowed his brow and looked at her. They'd been back at the apartment for only a few hours, but he couldn't seem to get the antsy feeling out of his system. His police issue phone buzzed in his pocket again. *Damn.* Wallace wanted him to move, to get the goods on Balthazar. She was too close to the fire. "Where did you want to go?"

"I know how to get up onto the roof." Jude grabbed his hand. "It's private and a good reason to get some fresh air."

Within minutes, they stood beside the fire door and stared at the skyline. Light cascaded around her shoulders. Ramon led her to the edge of the roof to sit along the wall. Instead, she straddled his lap like she might at the club. It wasn't a matter of intimacy, but more to pin him down...and he liked it. Blood rushed straight to his groin, but Jude didn't seem interested in sex. She acted like she needed to talk.

"You do realise someone could come up here, or, worse, lock us up here." Ramon forced a laugh and tried to take her face in his hands. Instead, she shied away. "What's wrong?"

"You've been acting screwy since you said the L word. Why don't you tell me what happened or whatever's on your mind? I don't want you to change your mind, but it happens. I'm a big girl and I can take it." Jude squirmed and tucked her hair behind her ears. "Start with your folks. I don't like to know I look like the woman who abandoned you. If it's clouding how you feel about me, I want to know."

Ramon stared out at the array of tall buildings and radio towers. Jude knew half of Drew's story already. She deserved to know the truth—who he really was and why he needed to bring Tiny down. He guessed she wanted his side, nothing more, nothing less. Except he couldn't talk about his real life. Then again…how could he tell her that his life and childhood weren't normal? How could he explain that he still couldn't deal with his past? Because Ramon Decker didn't have a screwy past, but he could talk about Drew's. He sighed and began to speak.

"I'm not who you think I am, but let me start at the beginning. You told me your story—here's mine. My father drank and Carol didn't want kids. He was a nineteen-fifties conservative. She was a hippie, complete with caftans and leather sandals. She was *too free* for us and he was extremely straight-laced. Their love affair was a good time and I was the accident that spoiled it. They got married because of me."

Ramon drummed her thighs with his thumbs and looked away. Bringing up the past killed his sex drive and constricted his throat. Overriding guilt over things he couldn't change rattled through his brain. Still, she made it easy to talk.

Jude took his face in her hands. "So you became his whipping post?"

Tears he wasn't ready to shed threatened the corners of his eyes. "Yeah. They fought all the time and Carol wanted to bail. When the girls came along, they were included in the beatings. I stepped in to keep them from getting hurt. As a result, I got the worst of it."

Jude clenched her teeth and slowly closed her eyes. Worry etched her face. Ramon could only imagine what she thought.

"I'm not thrilled you went through that, but I'm glad you told me." Jude dropped her hands. Her eyes searched his. "You needed the release, didn't you?"

The tension building between his shoulder blades lessened. The need to reveal his identity surfaced and he tried in vain to shove it back down to the pit of his stomach. "I don't know what I need, but bottling that up didn't help much." The words came out in a jumble.

Jude cocked her head. "So, who are you really? A master spy, or a runaway convict or something? Your accent isn't foreign or anything, and you talk with more eloquence than any bouncer I've known."

Ramon sighed heavily and looked away again.

Jude caught his face in her hands and brought his eyes to hers. "It won't change how I feel about you. You're special to me." The lines around her eyes softened and a smile curled the corner of her mouth.

With that, the Ramon façade melted. No more hiding—no more fear. He massaged her thighs with his strong hands. "I'm not a convict, but I've been known to spy."

Jude laced their fingers. Mirth coloured her voice. "You do strike me as a real wild child."

Ramon allowed a chuckle to slip past his lips. "I'm still a wild child...er...man."

Her voice dropped an octave. "You are."

Ramon kissed her nose. Damn, he hated being emotional. Whose idea had it been to bring up the past? He wasn't so sure he liked it. Jude wrapped her arms around him and Ramon pulled her even closer. "You make being wild fun."

"Good."

Ramon felt lighter, like the weight bringing him down had evaporated once and for all. At the same time, he had no idea what Jude was thinking because she simply smiled.

Instead, Jude smoothed his hair and continued to hold him close. "Whatever your secrets are, you're not alone. I won't leave you," she whispered. "You don't always have to be so tough." Her words tickled against his ear, making him shiver. Women just didn't affect him like that, but Jude could without trying. Her compassion scared him.

Ramon looked up. "I don't suppose you have any deep dark secrets you'd like to get off your chest?"

Jude grinned through her own tears. "You know all about me. My father's dead. My mother's in Cleveland raising her second family, and I'm a stripper trying to put myself through college." She stifled a giggle and chewed on her bottom lip. "Should I make something up? I'm not very good at fibbing, but I could try to conjure a doozy if it'd make you feel better."

Ramon paused to consider her words. She didn't let her past blot out what she wanted to do with her life. "No, you're special just the way you are."

Her grin grew. "Good, now tell me some really juicy stuff."

"Like what?"

"Food, radio stations, colour, song, TV shows, and hobbies—other than drawing," she said. She rubbed her pussy along his cock, making him weak in the knees despite the denim barrier. Amusement and smouldering sexuality sparkled in her eyes. "What are your favourites?"

Ramon couldn't help but grin along with her. Damn, he loved her blunt honesty.

"Greasy cheeseburgers, metal, the pale pink of your skin, anything by Korn, sports events, and dirt races." Ramon didn't need further convincing—he was head-over-heels in love. Lord, she made being in love so easy and natural. Now he needed to make her fall for Drew, not Ramon.

Jude slipped down between his knees and opened the fly on his jeans. "Art is one of my favourite things." Ramon sprang to attention in more ways than one. She pushed all his buttons and muddled his common sense. Blood pounded hotly through his veins. He clenched his hands on the edge of the wooden seat.

"Whoa."

Jude looked up only a moment. "I forgot to mention that I like this, too," she said huskily. His erection popped free from his boxers. A sexy smile graced her sweet face. In one smooth stroke, she took him to the back of her throat and sucked greedily. Her skills improved by leaps and bounds each time she gave him pleasure.

Ramon groaned and gripped the bench. Her action took him by surprise and made it hard to think straight. Any fleeting thought of moving on without her went right out the window. Jude's lips felt sinful as she took her time, savouring, sipping him. She could torment with the best of them. "God, woman, you're perfect."

Jude continued to pump her hot wet mouth up and down on his cock, bringing him to the brink before switching speeds to prolong the climax. He felt like a horny cad and she took the edge off by loving him. And damn it if he didn't like it.

Her tongue grazed along the thick vein on his penis. She winked and kissed the crown.

"Someone could...oh fuck," Words failed him and he gave into the heady sensations. "Oh, what the hell..." He gripped her hair and guided his orgasm. He didn't want it to end, but he needed finish. What a sweet conflict.

Jude hummed her approval. Before he came, she slithered up along his stomach and dropped her jeans, displaying her bare ass to the entire skyline. God, he needed to break her nudist tendencies, well at least when they were in public.

"Take me here on this roof," Jude whispered and straddled his dick. The wetness between her legs lubricated their union. "Who cares who sees us?"

Ramon ran a hand along her slick folds. Damn, she was horny. "I didn't bring along any condoms." He whimpered. Forget observers—he had damn poor planning skills.

Jude moved up and down on his cock, increasing her arousal and making him crazy with desire. Her clit thrummed a heady beat against his willing dick. What was wrong with him? He should be thinking about her, not her taking care of his selfish needs. Loving Jude wasn't part of the fucking operation.

Jude grasped his shoulders. "Come inside me, Ramon. I'm inexperienced, but I'm not stupid. I'm on the pill. It's fine."

Ramon nearly stopped breathing. What he'd waited for all his life was in the palm of his hand. *Jude*. He ripped her T-shirt over her head and pulled the straps of her bra down, exposing her breasts to the cool morning air. With his thumbs, he flicked her nipples.

Jude threw her head back and moaned. "Yes, yes."

Something raw and animal took over. "I want you to bear my children," he growled and raked his fingers down her back. "I want you for the rest of my life." Ramon felt the primal urge to mark her as his own and claimed her shoulder, leaving a love bite — purple to mix with the cream.

She gasped. "Yes."

His hands clasped her hips and dictated the speed of intercourse once the orgasm hit. Jude shuddered in his arms, but didn't back away. Her hair fell in wisps around her face. Jude collapsed boneless in his arms, thoroughly fulfilled. Ramon loved that he could do that to her so easily. Everything felt right. Now to tell her who he was.

Finally, their breathing returned to normal. Jude felt like she'd just come down from a fantastic journey. Ramon knew her body so well and a mere caress reduced her to a steaming puddle in his arms. Not that she complained.

Ramon rubbed her shoulder. "We should get back to town. I have to work tonight."

Jude nodded. "Me, too. I guess the industry won't take a break because we found each other, will it?"

"No."

Ramon slid the straps back up onto her shoulders and found her shirt. Just like the gentleman she knew he was. They both stood while she adjusted her clothing to look presentable.

"Babe, we need to talk."

"Haven't we been talking all this time?" Her hands trembled, but she winked to hide her trepidation. He'd changed the subject so fast..."Well, when we weren't making love."

"There's something I've got to tell you."

Her blood ran hot and cold. Whatever he had to say could be good or it could be very bad. "Like?"

His shoulders slumped and he stared at her hands. "I don't know how to say this."

"Say it." She placed her hand on his. "Whatever it is, we'll get through it together."

"I can't see you anymore."

She scurried off his lap and toppled onto the ground. "What?"

"Honey, there's so much you know about me, but you don't know me."

"Tell me?" She stood and finger-combed her hair, unsure of what else to do. Gulping air to breathe, she began to pace. The same old fear reared its head. Something she loved, something she wanted couldn't be hers because of her past or her profession. She shook her head. She wasn't going to crumble until she'd heard everything. "Start at the beginning and tell me whatever the hell is going on because I really need to know what the fuck is happening."

Ramon's confidence withered but he continued to look her in the eye. "I need you to run. Far as you can away from me. I'll bring you down and you're a good girl."

"Ramon?" Jude took a step back and the world around her faded to nothingness as the severity of his words washed over her. "What are you saying?"

"My goddamned name isn't Ramon. It's Drew. Detective Drew Alwyn. The body you found was Sergeant Randy McCall, otherwise known as Slade McMann. He was one of my best friends and he's dead. I'm supposed to be outing Tiny and his drug trade, not everything else." His voice cracked. "Finding you, being with you, loving you—that wasn't part of the deal, but I'm not upset it happened."

Jude shoved both hands into her hair and backed farther away from him. She stared out at the skyline and forced the tears to remain at bay. Corey's ridiculous remarks hadn't been so ridiculous after all. He'd known about Ramon-slash-Drew, the cop. She tapped her foot with nervous energy. All the things that had happened, all the lies, the shams...

Astra and Slade-slash-Randy hadn't had to die and all along Ramon had known... Drew had known... Whatever.

"Jude?"

She wrapped her arms around her body and drew a long breath into her lungs, letting it out slowly. "You lied to me."

"I can't help it, sweetheart."

"Don't call me that." Bile rose in her throat and her stomach churned. First he said he loved her and now he told her he was a cop who knew Slade. Could he have saved Astra? *Shit.* What would happen when Tiny found out, if he didn't know already? She'd be next in the dumpster.

"Jude."

She turned around and stared at him. The rough-around-the-edges man she'd fallen in love with looked back at her, but the love she'd felt wasn't the same. All the things she'd kept bottled for so many years mixed with the anger, frustration and sadness. She balled her fists. "You knew and let me...*service* you. Like here. Was it to let Tiny see kink? Make him think what we were doing was real?" *God, please don't say it...* She covered her mouth with her hands and leaned against an air duct. "Whatever we were to you, it wasn't an act to me." The breeze whipped a lock of her hair across her brow. "It was never a joke."

Ramon closed the gap between them and tipped his head. "I kept getting rid of the cameras because I cared about you. Still do care. Jude, Tiny's trying to ruin your life. What you do in your own room is your business—not his." He smoothed a lock of her hair from her face. "I don't regret what happened between you and me. What we did was once in a lifetime."

Her heart splintered in her chest and the unshed tears finally slipped down her cheeks. "You say that now. What is the truth, then? Pity? To fit in and say you fucked a topless dancer?"

"Nothing like that. I saw you one night when I was casing the Silver Steel and couldn't get you out of my head." A smile curled on his lips, despite the rough tone in his voice. "You've invaded my dreams. I have a drawing I did of you, too. From memory."

Jude covered her face in her hands and dropped to the gravelly surface of the roof. The one man she shared a definite link with, and it was all about to go to hell.

"Everything else that's happened has been because I wanted it to, not to have a good cover or to pull the wool over your eyes." Drew knelt next to her and twined his fingers with hers. "When I said I loved you, I meant it. I'm scared you're going to get hurt because of me."

She drew air into her lungs, despite the burn. If he had to do this, had to walk away in order to do something greater than the both of them, then fine. Her pride would mend later. Jude stood and brushed the dust from her jeans legs. "I'm going downstairs — alone."

"Okay." Drew rose to his full height and nodded once.

She placed her hand over his heart. A final gesture for a broken love. "You never met me."

"Babe, don't do this."

"Don't?" She pulled her hand away and clenched it against her chest. "I fell in love with you...then you tell me not to see you. Now that I'm breaking as cleanly as I know how, you don't want it? Come on. Which do you want? Me to leave, or me to stick around until the sting is over? I'm trying to make this a little easier on the both of us by doing what you want." She stared out over the smattering of rooftops. "I'm trying."

"Part of me wants you to run as far away from me as you can so you don't get hurt. The rest of me wants you right on my side, helping me kick his ass straight to jail. You mean too much to me to put you in any more danger." He wrapped his arms around her from behind and rested his chin on her shoulder. "Look, I think we can pull this off if you trust me and do what I tell you."

"Damn it." She wiped the tears from her cheeks. She didn't have much choice. Either way she'd lose him. At least they'd go down working together. "What do I have to do?"

"You're going to go downstairs. Get ready for work like normal, drive in and pretend we've had an argument. Slam doors...scream if you want. I'm an asshole and you don't care about me any longer." He turned her around in his embrace. "If Tiny asks, I broke your heart and you want my head on a platter. I won't buy your goodies or something. Anything. He's wise to me and I can't dick around any longer. The team wants to move, whether I've got my love life in order or not."

"He'll kill you."

"Nah, I'll make the buy. He's dying to sell to me, to break me in. I'll say I'm trying to get over you."

"And this will work? You'll be safe?"

"Just hate me for now. I can't tell you the rest."

She closed her eyes. Simply hating him wasn't going to be enough, but with her heart in his hands, she had no choice. "I'll do it, but we're through."

Chapter Eleven

Ramon threaded his fingers together behind his head and waited outside Tiny's office. The last four hours had been sheer hell. Each time Jude danced, he yearned to cover her up and take her home. Seeing the venom in her eyes, real or rehearsed, didn't help. He tapped his foot. If things went to pot, he needed her to know he really cared. Stupid or not, he pulled his cell from his pocket and wrote a text message.

Corey cleared his throat and stepped beside the open door. "Mr Balthazar will see you now. Weapons?"

"You know I do. Standard issue for the club." He flashed the gun in his shoulder holster. "Be prepared in case someone gets fucked up."

"I'll take it." Corey waggled his fingers. "Standard procedure in case someone fucks things up."

Ramon fought the urge to hesitate, to draw his weapon on Corey. It wasn't justifiable. He hadn't been fired upon first. *Fuck.* He slapped the gun into Corey's hand. "Happy?"

"Very."

With Corey behind him, Ramon entered Tiny's office. Unlike the shabbiness of the club, the wood-panelled room spoke of money and prominence. Cherry moulding and wide mirrors adorned the wall behind Tiny's desk.

"Like that?" Tiny stood and offered his hand. "Decorated myself. I like to think I've got a knack for design. But that's not why you're here, to admire my style. I hear you've been an asshole to one of my girls."

"We split."

"Uh-huh." Tiny nodded and folded his hands. "Judy is hard on the heart. Not as hard as some, but I can see where you're coming from. She's not one to walk away from. You had someone on the side?"

"I liked my blow better than her. She got pissed."

"Now, why didn't I know you had the habit?"

"I keep it quiet so I won't get the sack." Ramon glanced over his shoulder. "I shouldn't while I'm on duty, but I need some stuff. I'm hurtin' bad."

"From me?" Tiny's eyes shimmered. Delight? Greed? Ramon wasn't sure, but his hackles rose.

"Corey, let's get this boy one of the best."

"Affirmative."

Panic skated up Ramon's spine. Affirmative? *Fuck.* He opened his mouth to speak, but a blinding light flashed before his eyes and what felt like a spike ran straight through his brain.

"Only the best."

Ramon swayed on his feet. He had to stay awake. Had to bring this bastard down. Had to... His knees weakened. Had to keep his eyes open. He blinked as his vision blurred. Had to...sleep...

* * * *

"Wake up, pretty boy."

A heavy foot kicked Ramon awake. His head throbbed. How long had he been out? The floor made a lousy bed and his muscles tightened in response. Fuck the façade... If he made it out, he wanted to be remembered by his name, not his damned cover.

"You're hurtin', but you ain't a pussy. Get up."

Drew swayed and forced himself into a sitting position. Crimson flowed into his eyes. Fuck...fresh blood. He wondered if Jude had got his message and was on her way to the station. He needed her to be. In his mind, a fuzzy image of Jude appeared in a flowing white dress. Curls cascaded around her face and down her shoulders. She smiled and held her arms open. *'I'm trying,'* she said and nodded her head. *'Stay okay.'*

Nothing like asking for the moon and stars from a fantasy...

"Do you really think I'd let you die that easily, Alwyn? Yeah, I know you're a goddamned cop."

Drew's eyes barely focused on Balthazar and his sharp tone.

Thwack!

Drew looked through his own blood at Balthazar, who'd used the pistol once more as a club. He felt delirious and couldn't begin to form words. Teeth were definitely loose from the repeated impact.

"I can't find your buddy, but Carlie told me he's here. You coppers never work alone." Balthazar laughed. "Guess she found your old lady... She wasn't impressed and said you traded down. Too bad because Carlie had the hots for you, even if she's a cop, too."

Through a blackened eye, Drew glared at Balthazar. He remembered Carlie's penchant for drugs. There was the link. How did he not see her using? Right—he was supposed to be high. *Damn it.*

Balthazar continued to laugh at Drew. "Your old lady can't save your lousy hide," he cackled. "You'll be dead by morning. I hope she looks good in black. Maybe I'll stop by for another dance."

Drew wanted to beat the hell out of Balthazar. What had he done to Jude? Knowing Jude had ever given Tiny private dances soured Drew's stomach.

A black and white vision of Jude wiggling her hips for Balthazar invaded his mind. Dressed only in a thong, Jude fondled and caressed herself while the dealer placed money at her feet. Drew wanted to scream her name. Private dances were part of the job, yes, but that knowledge didn't make the visual in his head any easier to take.

Thwack!

Drew's temple burned. Balthazar's voice broke him from the nightmare. "Who is your partner? Nester isn't here. Tell me if you want any chance of living through this... I *will* use Judy Blue Eyes against you. She's a decent piece of ass—not great, but decent and she'll look absolutely fucking fantastic in the compactor with Astra and Slade."

Drew's facial expression stayed as blank as possible with a broken jaw and a black eye. The tape remained in place, reducing his ability to answer. Inside, he seethed. Drew closed his eyes and tried to shake the feeling of disgust. He didn't want to think of Jude dancing for anyone but him. She wasn't a toy for sharing—she was *his* Jude and much more than a so-called decent piece of ass to be killed because Balthazar demanded blood. *Damn it.*

Drew wanted to scream. He wanted to fight. He wanted Jude.

Balthazar stopped laughing long enough to study Drew. "Alwyn, you know, we aren't that different. We both take scum off the street. Mine are junkies and yours are strippers. Maybe you should've quit the force to work for me. You two could've been very happy together without risking your jobs." He kicked Drew once more, leaving him in a crumpled ball on the floor.

"Spend your next few hours praying. God's the only one who can save your fucking soul now," Balthazar thundered and locked the door.

Drew fought the urge to sleep. Irrational thoughts moved into his brain. He pictured Jude laughing and lounging with Balthazar. The taste of iron in his mouth brought Drew back to reality. Jude wouldn't want anything to do with the dealer.

I need to stay alert.

Drew tried like hell to remain vigilant, but his injuries were too extensive and he succumbed to sleep. His last thoughts were of Jude.

I love you, babe...

* * * *

Drew awoke to voices. He didn't know where they were coming from, only that they were growing louder. How long had he been out this time? Bits and pieces of the conversation sounded like plans. Drew strained to comprehend the words, thankful to be alive. Or was it an argument? He wasn't sure.

"Shit. They're storming the joint. Knock off the fucker. They won't mess with us if we knock him off."

"I'm not having a cop-killing on my record."

"He ain't no cop."

Drew's ears perked up and his head throbbed.

"I'm not taking him out."

"He ain't worth the needle."

Seconds passed in silence. Someone was in the process of planning his execution. Drew saw nothing in the dark. Seconds turned into silent minutes filled with dread. Had Jude helped? Did she know about Balthazar? Had they killed Jude? *God...Jude.*

For a split second, Drew forgot what Jude looked like and that scared him the most.

The sound of gunshots rang in his ears. Garbled voices sounded like surrender, but Drew couldn't be sure. A loud crack against the one wall sent debris crashing down on his nearly prone body. Drew strained to hear more gunshots and shouting. Were they giving up? Did Balthazar have Jude? He prayed they wouldn't hurt Jude.

The gunfire wasn't in his room, but getting closer.

At that instant, Jude's face came into sharp focus. Relief washed over his body. If Drew was about to die, at least his last thoughts would be of her.

More gunfire thundered around him. *Who's shooting?* He prayed the bullets wouldn't hit him—he needed to get home to Jude. Moments later, Drew saw a shaft of light under the door. "You check in there! He's gotta be around here somewhere! Come on—I can't lose him like this. I won't!"

Drew recognised the voice. Mateo. His mind whirled. Was Jude far behind? Was she safe? Was she dead?

A clunk on the door increased the light in the room. Figures piled into the small space. Mateo began to fling debris around the room. His face lost all colour when he saw Drew. "Get in here! We got an officer down," he screamed. "Drew? Drew, talk to me."

Drew wanted to reply. With his jaw broken and tape sealing his mouth, it was impossible. Instead, he lifted his head and the room span. Nausea washed over his body. It was all too much, too soon. Once outside and properly medicated, Drew would gladly spill his guts. Right now he wanted out of the house and into Jude's arms.

"Officer down! Officer down. He's still alive," Mateo screamed and knelt next to Drew. He untied the cord from Drew's wrists and gently unpeeled the silver tape. "I don't know how you got through this, but I'm proud of you, buddy. They got Balthazar in custody. He gave up after a bullet to the right shoulder, courtesy of yours truly."

Drew took a deep, ragged breath while Mateo continued his questions. "How did you get to her? She said a text… You loved her or some shit. Where's the phone?"

Weakly, Drew opened his coat. The cracked device dropped to the floor with a clunk. He grunted a reply and leaned his head on the floor. It hurt to breathe. Everything hurt.

Mateo grinned. "It was damn stupid, but it got you out. I applaud you for it."

As Mateo spoke, the stretcher arrived with Lieutenant Wallace in tow.

"Good job, officer. Good job, both of you. Get him out to the ambulance," Wallace instructed as the paramedics entered the room.

Drew's head lolled on his shoulders. If he died from the damned beating, he wanted to see Jude first.

Outside, Jude paced next to the ambulance. The urge to scream caught in her throat. An armed officer stood guard next to her. Time ticked by so slowly, she felt things reverted to slow motion. She knew there was nothing she could contribute and the desire to help riddled her with nervous energy. She shoved her shaky fingers through her dishevelled hair, then scrubbed them over her face.

Please let him be okay. God, please save him. Then she'd kick his butt.

What seemed like an eternity passed before she saw any movement outside the house. Police officers escorted fifteen or so men and women in handcuffs out of the establishment. Jude wondered if it was over. She looked for Drew among the upright individuals.

A barrage of gunshots split the air. Her heart twisted in her chest and her breathing stopped. Were they shooting at Drew? Was he shooting at them?

Jude sank to the floor of the vehicle. He was dead—she was sure of it.

Lights flashed and sirens blared. Through the chaos, she saw a large man with an enormous tattoo on his scalp leave the premises in handcuffs. He looked familiar.

That tattoo...a tribal design with a biochemical style monogram...

Oh, God. Her boss, Tiny Balthazar, drug lord extraordinaire. He'd tried to kill Drew.

"Stop pushing me," a woman screamed. Jude knew that voice too—it was Carlie. "You can't arrest me. I'm one of the cops. Those drugs weren't mine."

Through the ambulance window, Jude watched a scruffy man stuff Carlie into the back of a waiting cruiser. When the man saw Jude, a grin brightened his face. He crossed over to her position and tugged her out of the vehicle.

She hardly recognised him and shied back. He didn't look like the blond barrel of a man she knew. "Jude, it's okay. I'm James Mateo, Drew's partner. It's safe," Mateo said and hugged her. "You were brave to make that call to nine-one-one. Because of you, we upped the ante on the sting op and found Drew in time. We were able to arrest Balthazar, not only for the drug charges, but also the assault of a police officer, and the alleged murders of Sergeant Randall McCall and Astra Devlin. Drew was next on his hit parade."

Jude rocked back on her feet. Relief washed over her body, followed by a pang of fear as she further processed Mateo's statements. Someone would pay for the deaths of her friends.

"Next on what? Where's Drew?" She clutched Mateo's arm. Her eyes widened and her breath caught in her throat. "How bad is he hurt, James? Is he...dead?"

"It's not pretty, but he should manage. I assume you'll provide some 'special' nursing to get him up and running," Mateo said and dug his elbow into her ribs. He turned and nodded to the arriving stretcher. "Over there..."

Jude glanced in the direction of Mateo's nod. She nearly fainted. Drew's body was broken and bloody. His face swelled from the injuries, not to mention the matted, bloody hair and cuts marring his skin. A crash-test dummy looked more life-like.

Drew grinned weakly. He couldn't even raise his arm to wave. Her heart broke.

"You can ride in the ambulance along with us," the EMT said and helped her into the vehicle.

Jude nodded. She had to force her feet to move. Seeing Drew in such a bloody mess was devastating, but at least he was alive. As she climbed into the ambulance, Drew's faint grin gave her strength. If he could deal, then so could she.

She sat at Drew's feet and massaged his calf. In her mind, she thanked God for bringing him home. Though swollen and purple, he smiled. She knew this wouldn't be the last time he went undercover. He'd eventually be in another dangerous position—police work wasn't exactly secure in every situation. She thanked God that Drew had come home. She could be strong without him, but preferred to be strong together. She loved him too much to go it alone.

With the tip of his boot, Drew rubbed her thigh.

Jude smiled through her tears. At least he was alive and safe.

Chapter Twelve

Jude sat on the edge of the bed and flipped through her magazine. Drew glanced over at her, reading one of the headlines. The words 'hump', 'dance' and 'get his attention' certainly grabbed *his* attention. "Babe?" He bumped her shoulder. "What are you reading?"

He'd been out of the hospital for more than a week and his strength increased with each passing day, but man, the weight of recovery wore on him sometimes. His ribs ached and, when they didn't, his head throbbed. Getting beaten up sucked ass.

"Garbage. The magazine is garbage." She tossed the magazine aside. "The doctor told me to wait until you were back in the pink to antagonise you."

He crooked one brow and squeezed her thigh. "He's being cautious. Why?"

"There's a few things we need to iron out." Jude folded her hands and stared him in the eye. "Things that are crucial to the future."

The future. He sighed. Jude never ceased to surprise him. Normally her quirks didn't shock him to the core, but after seeing death head-on, well, he wasn't going to brush her off. "And you mean..."

"So, how *did* you hook up with Officer Carlie Kenworth?" Jude turned to face him, sitting cross-legged across from him. "I mean, a man of high standards, such as you should've known when to be on guard and with whom. We aren't all fine, upstanding citizens. She oozed trouble from every pore."

Drew sighed and reached out to caress Jude's thigh. "You'd be surprised."

Jude crossed her smooth legs over his and rested her head on his shoulder. "So?"

"The truth is that she looked like my ex-wife, Nat," Drew confessed finally. "I thought I needed someone to fill her place in my life. I was wrong."

"I see..." she said and trailed off. Jude smoothed her fingers along the slender silky patch of hair on his bare chest. The bruises were slowly fading, but the tenderness remained. She touched the outline of his ribs gingerly.

"It wasn't my brightest move, I'll agree. When we weren't arguing, we had... Well, it wasn't a good time. Actually, it was pretty awful dating a fellow officer. I guess I was too weak to walk away and she liked the attention. I met her at a bar. Martin introduced us."

Jude raised a brow and turned to look at him. "Was that before or after you two split?"

Drew snorted. "After."

Jude licked her lips and her eyes flashed. He could see the wheels in her mind turning overtime. What went through that beautiful mind of hers, this time?

A smile drifted across her lips.

"What?" Drew shifted uncomfortably. Jude knew every button and pushed with all her sexual might.

He was up to her challenge, if he could figure out what she was up to and could move in a way to incur the least amount of pain.

Jude's smile increased a thousand watts, making him squirm even more. "You won't make that mistake again," she purred and slid onto his lap. She shifted to rub her body on his growing heat.

Drew reached up to cup her face in his hands. "Absolutely not," he replied and brought her lips to his. What was meant to be a quick taste lingered into complete consumption—she tasted too damn good to turn away.

Jude rocked back and forth on his cock. "Ummm," she hummed in approval. "Drew, you'll make me forget what I practised telling you in the mirror."

"You used the mirror? Isn't that my job?" Through the tank top, he clasped her breasts in both hands. He relished the fact that she went braless just for his pleasure. He toyed with her nipples, cursing the constrictive cotton fabric. "So, what exactly were you rehearsing?"

Jude threw her head back and groaned. "You play dirty."

"Always. So, you came in here to tell me something." Drew continued to knead her pliable flesh. His mouth mauled her neck with heated kisses. "What was it?"

"Yes," she gasped. Her eyes rolled back and her lips parted. God, he loved when she zoned out, drugged by his movements.

As she tilted her head back, her long hair tickled his naked legs, sending shivers up his spine. His blood thrummed in his veins and his chest squeezed, not from pain, but pleasure.

"So?" Drew dropped his hands into his lap. Time to mess with her head. Turnabout was fair play. He pulled a condom from the nightstand and placed it on his lap.

Jude snapped back to attention and shook her head. Her hair fell in her eyes and her cheeks flushed, turning him on all the more. "You can't get off that easily...until I do."

Jude pulled his erection out of his boxers and wrapped it in the latex barrier. Drew slid her panties to the side, rubbing her wetness on his shaft. To add to her pleasure, he grazed his thumb across the tight nub of her clit. She panted. "Oh...you're not going to...tease me."

She shifted to accommodate him.

Drew grasped her hips, increasing their sexual rhythm. "We *will* get off and it *will* be incredibly easy," he groaned. "God, I love you, woman."

Jude moaned. Could she get any more responsive to his touch? Never...and he loved it that way.

"I love you too, Drew."

Hearing her say his name, not the cover name, thrilled him to his core. Drew ran his fingers through her hair to move it from her face. He needed to look into her piercing blue eyes—there he found strength, power and peace. Yes, she was truly his other half. Every time they made love, Jude proved their mutual devotion to each other was real and oh so strong.

Jude dug her nails into his thighs as the climax wracked her body.

"Yes," he hissed, giving way to his own orgasm. "Yes, babe... Come for me."

Jude screamed his name. "Drew! Oh, God! Drew!"

Drew beamed inwardly. He could listen to the music of her soul every day.

"Oh, Drew." Jude's sated body fell limply against his firm chest.

Drew winced at the momentary pain and cuddled her close. "Now, what was it that you had to tell me?" He ran his fingers through her silky hair. "I played dirty. Your turn."

"I bought a cat," she whispered in laboured breath. "Adopted him..."

Drew's brows bunched together as he processed her statement. Why did they need a cat? Hell, how had he not noticed?

"We need a cat so I have company while I'm here alone. With Gramma and your uncle in Florida... I didn't want to be lonely," Jude continued without raising her head. Her breath tickled his still-sensitive skin.

"That's why you have me," Drew said, still confused and engrossed in watching her breasts move in time with her heartbeat.

"When you're working, you can't be here." She sat up and grinned. "I got Sergeant Pepper from the APL. I didn't exactly plan to go there, but I drove past and had to stop in. The lady who runs the APL was so nice and I couldn't say no to the little guy. He was born there and looked so forlorn—I had to take him home."

Police theme? The Beatles? Didn't matter. Drew liked the name. He tipped her face to his. "Did the lady con you into naming him—it *is* a him, I assume—Sergeant Pepper? Or was there a better reason?"

Jude bit the corners of her mouth. "Well, you're a detective and I'm Jude, so I thought Sergeant Pepper just fit." She paused. "It was better than Walrus or Abbey or Eggman. Have you got a more suitable suggestion?"

Drew continued to mutely stroke her hair and consider her explanation. A cat would be decent company. Farms had cats. Lots of them. They caught mice and other rodents, didn't they? The barn cats had and left them everywhere. "So where is the good Sergeant?"

Jude sat up, pursed her lips and whistled. As if on cue, a rather skinny, mottled mahogany and white cat strolled into the room, stalked across the carpet and jumped up onto the bed.

Drew narrowed his eyes to size up the new member of the family. In turn, the little cat sat patiently on the end of the bed, doing the same to him. The scrawny devil had Matilda's spots and wasn't more than a year old. Food and a place to nap were the only things the cat cared about — and maybe some play time or a good scratch behind the ears.

"What if I'm allergic to him?" Drew held out his hand. The cat gave him a finicky sniff and plopped down on his side licking his paw as if he'd already lost interest.

"No dice," Jude replied and giggled. "I called Gramma. She told me you loved cats."

Drew sighed and pulled her close. Double teamed. Jude was too smart for his own good — not that he'd let on. "You got me. You win." He kissed her temple. Damn, he was thankful to have her in his life.

"I always had you." Jude sat up and grinned like a Cheshire cat. "Are you ready for surprise number two?"

Drew cocked his head. "Let me guess...a dog?"

Jude shook her head. "Too cliché." She slid off his lap and disappeared into the bathroom. When she returned, she held a small box. Her eyes sparkled with mischief and her smile was a country mile wide. Jude scooted onto the bed, next to him. "Ready?"

Drew nodded tentatively. He feared her news was something awful. What did she hide behind her smile?

"Here," Jude said and handed him a white stick. "Congrats."

Drew stared at her gift. A pregnancy test. The questions filled his mind and wrinkled his brow. Had they made a baby? They did have plenty of unprotected sex, but…was it possible? He didn't think he could get a woman pregnant. According to Nat, he was infertile…low sperm count or something. He looked at Jude for answers. "Are you sure?"

"Considering that's the third test, I'd say I'm pretty sure. I've never been preggo before and never had to worry about it." Jude cocked her head. Wide-eyed and chin quivering, she chewed on her bottom lip. "Second thoughts?"

Drew stared at the test for what seemed like an eternity. Thoughts swirled around in his head. He needed to process her information and his feelings. Having children with Natalie had been out of the question. Regardless, another thought occurred to him. Would he be the same type of father as his own? Would his children be afraid of him? His stomach wrenched. Would Jude change her mind about him, too?

The longer he thought, the more Jude sank back into her seat. She turned to exit the bed. Did she think he'd turn away? Insist on paternity tests or even an abortion? No.

Lack of preparation and comprehension on his part? Yes.

"Hold up, babe." Drew reached out to pull her onto his lap. The image of a little boy with a dark crew cut and a Popsicle dribbling down his chubby little hand standing next to a little girl with dazzling blue eyes and curls flashed in his mind. Children. His children.

"Are you sure?"

"I said I'd tested three times." Jude nodded. Tears glistened in her eyes. "I have a doctor's appointment for Tuesday, but I'm sure," she whispered in a virtually inaudible voice.

Drew caught her chin and brought her lips to his. "Then I couldn't be happier. It's perfect," he said and kissed her. His child with the woman of his dreams—Drew nearly cried for joy. "I... We can and will break the cycle...together. And to think it all started with a simple glance at the club."

When they surfaced for air, worry etched Jude's face again. The tears began to fall from her beautiful eyes. She shivered. "Are you sure?"

Drew grinned like a man in love...like a man who just found out that he'll be a daddy. He knew she feared the past would come back to haunt them, but this was their future and it was a one thousand watt future.

"Babe, I've never been so sure in all my life," he said and stroked her stomach. Drew pictured Jude on her side across the bed, teaching the little one about art and Daddy's job. It was a sweet mental image he'd cherish until it came true. "This is perfect—you, me, Sergeant Pepper and a little one on the way. What else can a man ask for?"

The smile returned to Jude's face, followed by more tears. These were tears of joy. "I was afraid you'd changed your mind," she gasped and cuddled against his shoulder.

"No," Drew reassured her and stroked her hair. "All I've ever wanted was a woman to love me, a family to care for, and a home for all of us. You've given me that and so much more. Babe, I love you."

Jude kissed his collarbone. "I love you, too."

Drew squared his shoulders. "So when is the due date? The farmhouse does have plenty of space, but I'd like to know how long I have until I have to round up Ray, Logan and Ned to help me build a swing set or a fort."

Jude began to laugh and met his lips for a kiss. "What about a princess castle?"

"Can you imagine big old Ray painting something pink? He'd rather chew off his foot." Drew chuckled at the vision of his friends with cans of pink paint, covering a massive castle. Things would be hairy at times. But, as long as he had Jude and they were together, it would be all right. "Since we're sharing, I have something for you."

"What do you have?"

Drew's kindness turned Jude on and made her heart swell. She smoothed down the flyaway strands of hair. She felt beautiful. "Are you pregnant, too?"

"Har." Drew fumbled in his discarded track short pocket and produced a diamond ring. The gem sparkled in the light of the setting sun. "I never knew I could love someone so deeply so quickly. I met you and my world tumbled upside down in every perfect way possible. I love you and want you to be mine forever. Will you marry me, babe?"

Jude's mouth fell open. The man of her dreams asking her to marry him—was it real? The odd compulsion to pinch herself came to mind. Sensory overload or something like that. She stared at his hand, the ring, then his face. All the love bursting in her chest was mirrored in his eyes. Yes, she'd marry him. Hell, she'd take a rocket ride to the moon if that's what he wanted.

"I can't imagine my life without you," he admitted. "Nor do I want to..."

Drew didn't need to beg—he had her heart.

"Um, here's where you tell me yes, no, get lost, drop dead, I'm so happy...take your pick?"

Jude nodded. Like she could fathom life without him, either. Now that she'd found him, wild horses couldn't drag her away. The blood coursed through her body. She felt like she was flying. God, it felt wonderful. "Yes, forever."

Drew took a breath and nodded. Jude could see the relief wash over his body. He grappled with her hand and placed the ring on her finger. She looked at her new jewellery and marvelled at its brilliance. "Where did you get this so quickly? I never saw you leave and no one save for the guys from the force has been in to visit."

Drew threw his head back and laughed, making her slightly uncomfortable. Jude felt like smacking herself on the forehead.

Real smart – question his motives. He must think I'm an ungrateful brat. Nice.

Jude bit the inside of her cheek. "What?"

"I just figured I'd get an 'it's so beautiful' or 'it's what I've always wanted'," he chuckled. "Are you afraid I stole it?"

The slightest nudge of her shoulder belied her calm exterior.

"Sweetheart, I'm a cop. I don't thieve."

Jude blushed. Now she felt incredibly dumb. Drew saw to the core of her fear—honesty or a lack thereof. She twined her fingers together, wondering what else might go wrong.

"I have no manners," she admitted and snuggled into his arms. "It's very beautiful. I love it and you, but I don't deserve either."

Drew snagged her up in a bear hug and kissed the top of Jude's head. He chuckled happily. "You absolutely deserve the best in life, but you'll have to settle for me."

Jude's heart started again. "I will gladly," she replied. "But how did you get this? We've been nearly inseparable."

Drew's grin widened, showing off his bright teeth. "Gramma slipped it to me when we first arrived. It was her mother's and she insisted I give it to you."

Jude uncoiled from Drew and proceeded to remove the ring. *Oh, no – no family heirlooms.* She didn't deserve something that belonged in the hands of a blood relative. Guilt and apprehension rested low in her belly.

"This isn't for me. It should go to one of your sisters," she said and tugged at it as it jammed on her knuckle. "Even if they don't want it, it's rightfully theirs."

Drew took her hand, kissed it, and slid the ring back into its position. "No, they didn't want it. It was too small and they wanted at least a full carat or bigger." Drew wrapped her up in his arms. "It's only half."

Jude's body warmed in his embrace. He smelled so good that she wanted to climb inside him and his safety. Drew's sisters didn't deserve him, but she'd make him see how special he truly was.

She frowned. "Are you sure they won't be upset? This should be theirs." Who could be so materialistic that they would overlook and refuse something so important? His family didn't make sense.

"They will be," Drew said firmly and clasped her hand. "But it was Gramma's to give away. Great-Gramma Buescher told her to wear it proudly unless she felt another member of the family deserved it. She chose you."

Jude looked down at the diamond decorating her hand. It looked so perfect. His sisters were stupid not to want a family heirloom. She felt honoured to receive something so precious.

A custom fit, just like Drew, she mused. *The perfect beginning to our love story.*

"So, now what?" Jude rubbed her cheek on his chest. "We wait three days and run off to Atlantic City?"

"I thought maybe we'd take a trip up to the courthouse. Ned's willing to marry us if you're interested."

"Yeah?"

"Yup."

"Then, let's go."

About the Author

I always dreamed of writing the stories in my head. Tall, dark, and handsome heroes are my favourites, as long as he has an independent woman keeping him in line.

I earned a BA in education at Kent State University and currently hold a Masters in Education with Nova Southeastern University.

I love NASCAR, romance, books in general, Ohio farmland, dirt racing, and my menagerie of animals. You can also find me at my blog

Wendi Zwaduk loves to hear from readers.

You can find her contact information, website details and author profile page at http://www.total-e-bound.com.

Total-E-Bound Publishing

www.total-e-bound.com

Take a look at our exciting range of literagasmic™ erotic romance titles and discover pure quality at Total-E-Bound.

CPSIA information can be obtained at www.ICGtesting.com
Printed in the USA
BVOW040024190712

295607BV00001B/23/P